William G Kingsland

Robert Browning: Chief Poet of the Age

New edition, with biographical and other additions

William G Kingsland

Robert Browning: Chief Poet of the Age
New edition, with biographical and other additions

ISBN/EAN: 9783337013066

Printed in Europe, USA, Canada, Australia, Japan

Cover: Foto ©Raphael Reischuk / pixelio.de

More available books at **www.hansebooks.com**

ROBERT BROWNING:

CHIEF POET OF THE AGE.

ROBERT BROWNING:

CHIEF POET OF THE AGE.

BY

WILLIAM G. KINGSLAND.

NEW EDITION,

With Biographical and other Additions.

London:

J. W. JARVIS & SON,

28, *KING WILLIAM STREET, STRAND.*

1890.

*** THE PORTRAIT of Mr. Browning is from the *last* Photograph of the Poet taken, and reproduced by photogravure by kind permission of Mr. W. H. Grove, 174, Brompton Road, S.W.

PRINTED BY S. AND J. BRAWN, 13, GATE STREET, HIGH HOLBORN, W.C

PREFACE.

I AM gratified to find that this book has been so favourably received as to call for a second edition; a circumstance which has afforded me the opportunity of correcting some errors, and of somewhat enlarging the scope of the work, and thereby adding, I would fain hope, to its usefulness. My main purpose has been to offer a sort of manual for beginners in the study of Browning. There are various treatises in existence dealing critically with the poems; but none, it seemed to me, specially intended as a guide to beginners. My object is, primarily, to call attention to the simplest of the poems, while remarking on the leading characteristics of the poet's genius, in the hope that the reader may be induced thereby to study the complete works of Robert Browning. Of course, for more advanced students, the " Handbook " of Mrs. Orr is *the* guide to the full understanding of Browning.

My thanks are due to Mr. J. T. Nettleship (the well-known animal painter), for some kindly criticism, to which I have given heed; also to Mr. Thos. J. Wise and Mr. P. Jenner

B

Weir; and in a special degree to my friend Miss C. G. Barnard, from whom I have received much valuable help, and who in America as in England has been untiring in her efforts to make known this little work. I had hoped to have obtained Mr. Browning's approval of this new edition ; but can now only record the kindliness and heartiness with which he granted his permission to use whatever extracts I required : on one occasion writing : "As for the poems you require, pray help yourself to them as liberally as you please"; and again : "I am most happy to allow as many extracts from my poetry as you please to make." I may here be pardoned for quoting a letter I received from the poet, on my forwarding him a copy of the first edition of this work, with an intimation that a large-paper copy would follow :

19, WARWICK CRESCENT, W.,

March 17th, 1887.

My dear Kingsland,

How can I be other than most grateful to you for your generous belief in me ?— unwarranted as it may be by anything I have succeeded in doing, although somewhat justified perhaps by what I would fain have done if I could. But it is now a long time indeed since I have been assured of your sympathy, and proud of your friendship. As for the book—it seems to me sufficiently pretty on the outside to require no "large paper" or other enhancement of its attractiveness. I have no doubt that whoever reads it will be the more disposed to think favourably of my general writings : your extracts are calculated to excite interest in the poems of which they are such good samples. . . . You know how happy I shall be to see you : meantime, and always, remember me as

Yours affectionately,

ROBERT BROWNING.

I have also to express my acknowledgments to Mr. R. Barrett Browning for the cordiality with which he renewed whatever permission I had received from his father to use the extracts I have quoted in the following pages.

January, 1890.   W. G. K.

ROBERT BROWNING.

BORN MAY 7, 1812; DIED DEC. 12, 1889.

O STRONG-SOUL'D singer of high themes and wide—
  Thrice noble in thy work and life alike,
Thy genius sweeps athwart a sea whose tide
  Heaves with a pain and passion infinite !—
Men's hearts laid bare beneath thy pitying touch ;
Strong words that comfort all o'erwearied much ;
Thoughts that inspire and mould our inner life,
Strengthen to bravely bear amid world-strife ;
And one large Hope, full-orbed as summer sun,
That souls shall surely meet when LIFE is won !

So round thy memory we our thanks entwine—
Men are the better for these songs of thine :
At eve thy muse did o'er us mellower swell —
Strong with the strength of life lived long and well.

ROBERT BROWNING.

I.

" THERE were giants on the earth in
those days!"—so will the student of
literature a century hence have to
exclaim, in looking back to the Victorian age :
and one of the last, as the greatest, of the race
is the poet who passed away on the evening
of December 12th, 1889, in the Palazzo
Rezzonico, at Venice. Suddenly snatched
from among us—as to our dim sight Robert
Browning seems to have been—it is as though
the light of our deepest life had gone out, and
we were left in darkness and eclipse. Some of
us owed so much to this man ; our best im-
pulses, our highest aspirations, our noblest
endeavours after good—these were all fed at
the perennial fount of his verse. He led us,
by no devious way, to God, Truth, Immortality ; and the debt we owe him is one that
cannot easily be repaid—save by keeping his
memory green, and "passing on" to others all
that we have received from him. Robert
Browning was beyond and before all things a
good man—true to himself and to God ; and
we who were admitted to his presence, knew
well his manliness and worth, as also the rare
fidelity of his friendship. All that he has been

to our England of to-day is perhaps hardly yet known, for he was pre-eminently the teacher of the teachers; but it is being realized, and the full greatness of the Man and the Poet will not long wait acknowledgment.

As it is, we can yet hardly realize that Robert Browning is dead. Yet he was surely happy in the last hours of his earthly sojourn, happy in the manner of his "passing"—no man happier. He died, it may truly be said, at his post—the final product of his regal brain before his eyes. It was, I think, sometime during the summer of last year that he said to me: "I cannot be idle—I shall die in harness: I have been writing some small things lately, but I want to write one or two more large works before I die." Brave words, but alas, though he died "in harness," the "larger works" he was not permitted to execute: not *here*, at least; yet, perchance, yonder, "behind the veil"—who can tell? To him, the passing into the Unseen was not death, but *life*. The writer of an interesting article concerning the Poet, in the columns of the *Glasgow Herald*, says: "It seems but a day or two ago that the present writer heard from the lips of Mr. Browning a mockery of death's pitiful vanity—a brave assertion of the glory of life. 'Death, death! It is this harping on death I despise so much,' he remarked with emphasis of gesture as well as of speech. 'This idle and often cowardly as well as ignorant harping!

Why should *we* not change like everything
else ? In fiction, in poetry, French as well
as English, and, I am told, in American art
and literature, the shadow of death—call it
what you will, despair, negation, indifference
—is upon us. But what fools who talk thus !
Why, *amico mio*, you know as well as I that
death is life, just as our daily, our momentarily,
dying body is none the less alive and ever
recruiting new forces of existence. Without
death, which is our crape-like churchyardy
word for change, for growth, there could be
no prolongation of that which we call life.
Pshaw ! it is foolish to argue upon such a
thing even. For myself, I deny death as an
end of everything. Never say of me that I
am dead !' "

I well remember, too, some few years since,
the vehemence with which he spoke on the
subject of personal immortality, " If there is
anything I hold to, it is *that :* why, I *know*
I shall meet my dearest friends again !" But,
indeed, with *Asolando* before us, there need be
no more said on this matter.

It is but natural, and to a certain extent
right, that all beginners in the study of the
writings of Browning, should now desire to
know something of his life apart from his work.
But there is little to say,—at the present time
at any rate,—concerning the incidents of his
outer life apart from the development of

his inner life, as recorded in his writings. Indeed, his life was part and parcel of his work, and one can hardly be dissevered from the other. Still there are certain landmarks which may be duly noted, and will prove of interest to the student. On the 7th of May, 1812, Robert Browning was born at Camberwell—then a suburb in the south of London, but now drawn into the vortex of districts which marks our modern metropolis. His father, (who died in 1866, at the age of 84), was a clerk in the Bank of England, and was a man of wide and varied culture. In *Asolando* there is a delightful bit of autobiography, where the poet tells us that his " father was a learned man and knew Greek,"and proceeds to narrate how the little boy of five years old was introduced to Homer. It was doubtless from his father that the future poet imbibed that love of classical literature which was to take so original a development in his later years. Comparatively early in life he wrote :

" How well I know what I mean to do
    When the long dark autumn evenings come ;
And where, my soul, is thy pleasant hue?
    With the music of all thy voices, dumb
In life's November too !

" I shall be found by the fire, suppose,
    O'er a great wise book, as beseemeth age,
While the shutters flap as the cross-wind blows,
    And I turn the page, and I turn the page,
Not verse now, only prose !

" Till the young ones whisper, finger on li
   ' There he is at it, deep in Greek :
  ' Now then, or never, out we slip
   ' To cut from the hazels by the creek
 ' A mainmast for our ship !

" I shall be at it indeed, my friends !
   Greek puts already on either side
 Such a branch-work forth as soon extends
   To a vista opening far and wide,
 And I pass out where it ends."

But it was getting towards the afternoon of his career ere the Greek plant blossomed into the lovely *Balaustion*.

Of the poet's childhood little is recorded. At an early age he began to rhyme, and by the time he had reached his twelfth year, had written a considerable quantity of verses, which were shown to the well-known Rev. W. J. Fox, and that gentleman at once recognized the genius of the lad, and pro- phesied his future greatness. The boy was educated first at a school at Peckham, kept by Rev. Mr. Ready ; afterwards receiving private tuition at home, and subsequently attending lectures at the London University. After this he paid his first visit to Italy—a visit destined to have far reaching influence on his after career. It appears that for some time the young poet was under the influence of Byron ; but about the year 1825, his mother purchased for him Shelley's *Adonais*,* and other works

---

* As verifying Browning's early intimacy with the writings of Shelley, the following extract from a letter

of his, at that time exceedingly difficult to
obtain. Shelley seems to have awakened the
true poetic instinct in the youth, for on October
22nd, 1832, Mr. Browning had finished his
first poem, *Pauline.* As was natural, this
performance was greatly admired at home,
and the money to print it was given to him
by an aunt—of whom Mr. Browning (in a
letter now before me), writes : " The beloved
aunt who helped me, as you rightly say, was
my Mother's own and only sister."

In 1833, the little book came out—published anonymously by Saunders and Otley,
at the price of 5s. It is needless to say that
Pauline failed to gain the ear of the public ;
but it was nevertheless at once recognized by
those best capable of judging of its worth.
Mr. W. J. Fox received it generously, and
wrote freely concerning it. In a number of
the *Repository* for 1833, he says : " The work
before us gave us the thrill, and laid hold of us
with the power, the sensation of which has

of the poet's, dated " March 3rd, 1886," may be
quoted :—" As for the early editions of Shelley, they
were obtained for me sometime before 1830 (or even
earlier), *in the regular way*, from Hunt and Clarke, in
consequence of a direction I obtained from the " Literary Gazette." I still possess *Posthumous Poems*, but
have long since parted with *Prometheus Unbound*,
Rosalind and Helen, Six Weeks' Tour, Cenci, and the
Adonais. I got at the same time, nearly, *Endymion*,
and *Lamia*, &c., just as if they had been published a
week before, and not years after the death of Keats."

never yet failed us as a test of genius. Whoever the anonymous author may be, he is a
poet. We felt certain of Tennyson, before
we saw his book, by a few lines which had
straggled into a newspaper; we are not
less certain of the author of ' Pauline.' " The
critic then proceeds to warn the anonymous
writer that, by the character of his work, he
must not look for popularity, nor expect to
make a hit or to produce a sensation ; but his
recognition of the intrinsic merits of the poem
was ample; and was the first welcome given
to Robert Browning into the world of literature.

Some twenty years after the publication of
Pauline, the late Dante Gabriel Rossetti
came upon a copy in the British Museum, and
at once divined it to be the work of Browning,
—a wonderful instance of the prescience of the
painter-poet.

So far as Mr. Browning was concerned,
Pauline was left to its anonymity for five
and thirty years ; till, in 1868, it was reprinted
in the collected edition of his works, which
were in course of issue by Messrs. Smith and
Elder, in six volumes. In a prefatory note,
Mr. Browning says : " The first piece [*Pauline*]
I acknowledge and retain with extreme re-
pugnance, indeed purely of necessity ; for not
long ago I inspected one, and am certified of
the existence of other transcripts, intended,
sooner or later to be published abroad : by

forestalling these, I can at least correct some misprints (no syllable is changed) and introduce a boyish work by an exculpatory word." But the lovers of Mr. Browning would not willingly let *Pauline* go—for not only is the poem a very beautiful one ; but it is interesting as revealing the bent of its author's mind from the beginning of his career.

The following, from a letter by Mr. Browning to Mr. Thos. J. Wise, in respect to *Pauline*, dated November 5th, 1886, will be of interest : " . . . The ' King ' is Agamemnon, in the tragedy of that name by Æschylus,—whose treading the purple carpets spread before him by his wife, preparatory to his murder, is a notable passage. The ' boy ' is Orestes, as described at the end of the *Choephoroi* by the same author. V. A. XX. is the Latin abbreviation of *vixi annos*, ' I was twenty years old,' that is, the imaginary subject of the poem was of that age."

In 1886, a facsimile of the original *Pauline*, edited by Mr. Thos. J. Wise, was brought out under the auspices of the *Browning Society*, and has now become a rare volume. When this re-issue was in contemplation, Mr. Browning was asked if he would kindly say a word of introduction, and he wrote :—" I really have said my little say about the little book already elsewhere,* and should only

---

* Presumably in the preface, from which an extract

increase words without knowledge. An introductory sentence or two of your own will be
better in every way. There was a note of ex-
planation in the copy I gave John Forster,—
which contained also a criticism by John Mill.
It is not included in the catalogue of his books,
however, but may turn up some day."

In 1834, Mr. Browning again set out on his
travels, spending some time at St. Petersburg.
His pen was not idle, however, for in 1835
appeared *Paracelsus*—and at a bound the
young poet took his position among the
leading spirits of the age. Still, as with
Pauline, the reading public and the critics
would have little to say to *Paracelsus*—though,
as with the former poem, the "few" saw and
acknowledged its power.

From the original preface to this work, the
poet would appear to have anticipated the
verdict of the "general reader," for he says:

"It is certain, however, that a work like mine
depends more immediately on the intelligence
and sympathy of the reader for its success ;—
indeed, were my scenes stars, it must be his
co-operating fancy which, supplying all
chasms, shall connect the scattered lights into
one constellation—a Lyre or a Crown."

Paracelsus brought him fame, and friends,
if nothing else; and in the Reminiscenses

is quoted above, to the six volume edition of his writings of 1868.—W. G. K.

of Macready, the reader will find various
notices of the poet and his first great work.

In 1837, Browning came before the public
as a writer of plays—his historical tragedy of
Strafford, being published by Messrs. Long-
man.   It was brought out at Covent Garden
on May 1 of that year.

It may be interesting to the modern reader
to give an extract from the original preface to
Strafford, and the reader will not fail to note
the passage I have taken the liberty of print-
ing in *italics*:

"I had for some time been engaged on a
Poem of a very different nature . . . .
and am not without apprehension that my
eagerness to freshen a jaded mind by di-
verting it to the healthy natures of a grand
epoch, may have operated unfavourably on
the represented play, which is one of Action
in Character, rather than Character in Action.
To remedy this, in some degree, considerable
curtailment will be necessary, and, in a few
instances, the supplying details not required,
I suppose, by the mere reader.   While a
trifling success would much gratify, *failure
will not wholly discourage me from another
effort: experience is to come; and earnest endeavour may yet remove many disadvantages.*
The portraits are, I think, faithful. . . . My
Carlisle, however, is purely imaginary.   I at
first sketched her singular likeness roughly in,

as suggested by Matthew and the memoir writers—but it was too artificial, and the substituted outline is exclusively from Voiture and Waller."

The play was, as I have said, produced at Covent Garden Theatre, on May 1, 1837 ; the *Literary Gazette* of May 6, of that year remarking that Macready's *Strafford* was forcible and striking : "Miss Faucit played with great taste and effect ; Vandenhoff's *Pym* was rather croaky. Messrs. Bennett and Webster did well for Hollis and Vane. The *King* (Dale), was awfully bad ; the Queen (Vincent) only a shade better." In connection with the statement that Browning's acted plays have always been failures, we may note the following from *The Examiner*, of May 14, 1837 : "*Strafford* was winning its way into even greater success than we had ventured to hope for it ; but Mr. Vandenhoft's secession from the theatre has caused its temporary withdrawal. It will be only temporary, we trust ; no less in justice to the great genius of the author, than to the fervid applause with which its last performance was received by an admirably-filled house."

About 1838, Mr. Browning would seem to have set to work in earnest on one of the most characteristic—as it is certainly the most debated — of his works. This was *Sordello*, which was published in 1840. This,

too, may be said to have fallen almost still-
born from the Press—though there were even
then not a few who recognized its glamour
and fascination. In 1863, this exotic poem
was revised and reprinted, with a dedication
to J. Milsand, of Dijon, one of the poet's ripest
friends, and a man of rare worth and discern-
ment. The dedication is worth noting here,
as much for the frankness of its self-criticism
as for the friendliness to which it gave
utterance :

" Let the next poem be introduced by your
name, and so repay all trouble it ever cost me.
I wrote it twenty-five years ago for only a
few, counting even in these on somewhat more
care about its subject than they really had.
My own faults of expression were many ; but
with care for a man or book such would be
surmounted, and without it what avails the
faultlessness of either ? I blame nobody, least
of all myself, who did my best then and since ;
for I lately gave time and pains to turn my
work into what the many might,—instead of
what the few must—like ; but after all, I
imagined another thing at first, and therefore
leave as I find it. The historical decoration
was purposely of no more importance than a
background requires ; and my stress lay on
the incidents in the development of a soul :
little else is worth study. I, at least, always
thought so,—you, with many known and un-

known to me, think so,—others may one day think so."

When Mr. Browning re-issued *Sordello*, as above stated, in 1863, many students were under the impression that it had been re-written, more especially as the poet had introduced, on each page, a series of explanatory head-lines. This theory as to the "re-writing" would appear to be still held in many quarters, but the following extract from a letter of Mr. Browning's will set the matter at rest :—

"I don't understand what —— can mean by saying that *Sordello* has been ' re-written : ' I did certainly at one time intend to re-write much of it, but changed my mind,—and the edition which I reprinted was the same in all respects as its predecessor—only with an elucidatory heading to each page, and some few alterations, presumably for the better, in the text, such as occur in most of my works. I cannot remember a single instance of any importance that is ' re-written,' and I only suppose that —— has taken project for performance, and set down as ' done ' what was for a while intended to be done."

In 1841, appeared the first of the series of poems entitled *Bells and Pomegranates*, in yellow paper covers, and issued first at sixpence ; the price being afterwards raised to a shilling. *Pippa Passes* formed the first number, and may surely be spoken of as the most

C

wonderful sixpennyworth ever offered to the reading public; it was dedicated in the following preface to Mr. Serjeant Talfourd :

" Two or three years ago I wrote a play, about which the chief matter I much care to recollect at present is, that a pitfull of good-natured people applauded it. Ever since, I have been desirous of doing something in the same way that should better reward their attention. What follows I mean for the first of a series of dramatical pieces, to come out at intervals, and I amuse myself by fancying that the cheap mode in which they appear will for once help me to a sort of pit-audience again. Of course, such a work must go on no longer than it is liked ; and to provide against a certain and but too possible contingency, let me hasten to say now what, if I were sure of success, I would try to say circumstantially enough at the close, that I dedicate my best intentions most admiringly to the author of *Ion*—most affectionately to Sergeant Talfourd."

In the following year (1842) were published Nos. 2 and 3, the former containing *King Victor and King Charles,* and the latter *Dramatic Lyrics,* consisting of the *Cavalier Tunes, Italy* (afterwards called *My Last Duchess*), *France* (now known as *Count Gismond*), *Camp and Cloister* (subsequently entitled *Incidents of the French Camp,* and

Soliloquy of the Spanish Cloister), In a Gondola, Artemis, Waring, Rudel and the Lady of Tripoli, Cristina, Madhouse Cells (Johannes Agricola, and *Porphyria's Lover), Through the Metidja to Abd-el-Kadr,* and *The Pied Piper of Hamelin.* No. 4 was issued in 1843, and contained that fine tragedy *The Return of the Druses;* and in the same year came No. 5, consisting of *A Blot in the Scutcheon,* which was produced at Drury Lane Theatre on the 11th of February, 1843, Miss Helen Faucit playing Mildred Tresham ; Mr. Phelps afterwards reviving the play at Sadler's Wells Theatre.

Concerning this tragedy, there is in Forster's *Life of Dickens,* a letter from the great novelist,—to whom Forster had lent the play in manuscript,—well worth quoting. Dickens writes :

" Browning's play has thrown me into a perfect passion of sorrow. To say that there is anything in its subject save what is lovely, true, deeply affecting, full of the best emotion, the most earnest feeling, and the most true and tender source of interest is to say that there is no light in the sun, and no heat in the blood. It is full of genius, natural and great thoughts, profound and yet simple, and yet beautiful in its vigour. I know nothing that is so affecting, nothing in any book I have ever read, as Mildred's recurrence to that : ' I was so young—I had no mother.' I know no love like it, no passion like it, no moulding of a splendid thing after its conception, like it. And I swear it is a tragedy that *must* be played; and must be played, moreover, by Macready. There are some things that I would have changed if I could (they are very slight, mostly broken lines); and I assuredly would have the old servant *begin his tale upon the scene ;* and be taken by the throat, or drawn upon, by his master, in its commencement. But the tragedy I shall never forget, or less vividly remember than I do now. And if you tell Browning that I have seen it, tell him that I believe from my soul there is no man living (and not many dead) who could produce such a work."

In 1844 came No. 6, consisting of *Colombe's Birthday*, and was dedicated to Barry Cornwall. This beautiful play was produced at the Haymarket on April 25, 1853,—Miss Helen Faucit playing *Colombe*. The following year No. 7 was issued—the price this time being two shillings; and was entitled *Dramatic Romances and Lyrics*, was dedicated to John Kenyon, and contained *How they brought the Good News from Ghent to Aix, Pictor Ignotus, Italy in England* (afterwards *The Italian in England*), *England in Italy* (known afterwards as *The Englishman in Italy*), the *Lost Leader*, the *Lost Mistress, Home Thoughts from Abroad, The Tomb at St. Praxed's, Garden Fancies, The Laboratory,*

The Confessional, The Flight of the Duchess, Earth's Immortalities, Song, The Boy and the Angel, Night and Morning, Claret and Tokay, the first part of *Saul, Time's Revenges,* and the *Glove.*

In the same year followed the last of the *Bells and Pomegranates,* No. 8, containing *Luria* and *A Soul's Tragedy.* This last issue was published at half-a-crown, and was dedicated to Walter Savage Landor.

Landor replied in his characteristic yet kindly fashion: "Accept my thanks for the richest of Easter offerings made to any one for many years. I staid at home last evening on purpose to read *Luria,* and if I lost any good music (as I certainly did) I was well compensated in kind. To-day I intend to devote the rainy hours entirely to *The Soul's Tragedy.* . . . . Go on and pass *us* poor devils ! If you do not go far ahead of me, I will crack my whip at you and make you spring forward."

The prefatory note to *A Soul's Tragedy,* not having been reprinted, it may be interesting to quote it here :

" Here ends my first series of *Bells and Pomegranates,* and I take the opportunity of explaining, in reply to inquiries, that I only meant by that title to indicate an endeavour towards something like an alternation, or mixture, of music with discoursing, sound with

sense, poetry with thought ; which looks too
ambitious, thus expressed, so the symbol was
preferred.   It is little to the purpose, that
such is actually one of the most familiar of
the many Rabbinical (and Patristic) accepta-
tions of the phrase ; because I confess that,
letting authority alone, I supposed the bare
words, in such juxtaposition, would sufficiently
convey the desired meaning.   ' Faith and good
works ' is another fancy, for instance, and perhaps no easier to arrive at : yet, Giotto placed
a pomegranate fruit in the hand of Dante, and
Raffaelle crowned his Theology (in the *Came-
ra della Segnatura*) with blossoms of the same ;
as if the Bellari and Vasari would be sure to
come after, and explain that it was merely
' *simbolo delle buone opere—il qual Pomograna-
to fu però usato nelle vesti del Pontifice appresso
gli Ebrei.*'—R. B."

Such were the *Bells and Pomegranates*—
poems which marked a new era in English literature ; and which I have enumerated in de-
tail that the reader, if he cares, may com-
pare them with the poems as published in the
collected edition of Mr. Browning's works.   I
may here remark that the ostensible reason of
their first publication in the above form was
that their author, seeing the public were
but little inclined to buy his books, and with
the knowledge of the expense his father had
already gone to in that direction, consulted

with his then publisher, Mr. Edward Moxon, who suggested the publication in pamphlet form, as the expense would thereby be considerably lessened.

It was in 1846, on September 12th, that a unique ceremony was witnessed in Marylebone Parish Church,—Elizabeth Barrett Barrett giving her hand in marriage to Robert Browning. " Among the few living poets of whom Elizabeth Barrett was wont to speak and write with admiration," says Mr. Ingram, " was Robert Browning. He had been characteristically mentioned in *Lady Geraldine's Courtship* and from that time forward his name and reputation found frequent mention in her correspondence." The " mention," in Miss Barrett's poem was, one may say, intuitive, for it gave, in a line, the leading motive of Mr. Browning's work :

" Or from Browning some ' Pomegranate,' which, if
    cut deep down the middle,
Shows a heart within blood-tinctured, of a veined
    humanity."

From this period, one may say that the story of their lives can best be known by their writings, the record of their personal history being a sealed book to the outside world ; but here and there some interesting peeps into their life are afforded us. After their marriage, they resided in Italy, this step being necessitated chiefly by the fragile health of Mrs. Browning. Pisa, was I believe, their first

abode, but they subsequently removed to
Florence, that fair city becoming the one home
of their married life. In *Old Pictures in
Florence*, Mr. Browning says :

"The morn when first it thunders in March,
　　The eel in the pond gives a leap, they say :
As I leaned and looked over the aloed arch
　　Of the villa-gate this warm March day,
No flash snapped, no dumb thunder rolled
　　In the valley beneath where, white and wide
And washed by the morning water-gold,
　　Florence lay out on the mountain-side.

" River and bridge and street and square
　　Lay mine, as much at my beck and call,
Through the live translucent bath of air
　　As the sights in a magic crystal ball."

For something like sixteen years they lived
in Florence—'Casa Guidi ' their home,—an
ideal home, wherein two poets lived and worked
in the completest love and harmony. Various
pictures have been presented to us of the home-
life of the Brownings in Italy, the best perhaps being that of Mr. Story, the American
sculptor. "We can never forget," he says,
" the square ante-room, with its great picture
and pianoforte, at which the boy Browning
passed many an hour—the little dining-room
covered with tapestry, where hung medallions
of Tennyson, Carlyle, and Robert Browning
—the long room filled with plaster casts
and studies, which was Mr. Browning's retreat
—and, dearest of all, the large drawing-room,

where *she* always sat. It opened upon a balcony filled with plants, and looked out upon the iron grey church of Santa Felice. There was something about this room which seemed to make it a proper and especial haunt for poets. The dark shadows and subdued light gave it a dreamy look, which was enhanced by the tapestry-covered walls, and the old pictures of saints that looked out sadly from the carved frames of black wood. Large bookcases, constructed of specimens of Florentine carving selected by Mr. Browning, were brimming over with wise-looking books. Tables were covered with more gaily-bound volumes, the gifts of brother authors. Dante's grave profile, a cast of Keats' face and brow taken after death, a pen-and-ink sketch of Tennyson, the genial face of John Kenyon, Mrs. Browning's good friend and relative, little paintings of the boy Browning—all attracted the eye in turn, and gave rise to a thousand musings. A quaint mirror, easy chairs and sofas, and a hundred nothings that always add an indescribable charm, were all massed in this room. But the glory of all, and that which sanctified all, was seated in a low armchair near the door, a small table, strewn with writing materials, books and newspapers, was always by her side."

In "Passages from the French and Italian Note-books of Nathaniel Hawthorne," the reader will find many references to Mr. Brown-

ing and his Italian home, the American writer
remarking that, " Mr. Browning's grasp of the
hand gives a new value to life, revealing so
much fervour and sincerity of nature.   He is
a most vivid and quick-thoughted person, logi-
cal and common-sensible."

Mr. Bayard Taylor, writing in 1851, says:
" Calling one afternoon in September at De-
vonshire Street, I was fortunate enough to find
the Brownings at home, though on the eve of
their return to Florence.   Browning received
me with great cordiality.   He was then, I
should judge, about 37 years of age, but his
dark hair was already streaked with gray about
the temples.   His complexion was fair, with
perhaps the faintest olive tinge, eyes large,
clear, and gray, nose strong and well cut,
mouth full and rather broad, and chin pointed
though not prominent.   His forehead broad-
ened rapidly upwards from the outer angle of
the eyes, slightly retreating.   The strong indi-
viduality which marks his poetry was expressed not only in his face and head, but in
his whole demeanour.   He was about the
medium height, strong in the shoulders but
slender at the waist, and his movements expressed a combination of vigour and elasticity."

The record of Browning's life at Florence
would be incomplete without some reference
to Walter Savage Landor.   It was to Robert
Browning that the " old lion " went in his
deepest trouble ; and to the younger poet's

judicious guidance the elder was ever amenable. Landor never failed to speak of of the kindness and innate courtesy of the Brownings—and the closing days of his chequered career were certainly made the brighter and happier through the sympathy and goodwill of Mr. Browning.

It was in the year 1850 that Mr. Browning published his chief religious poems—*Christmas Eve* and *Easter Day.* These works were written at Florence ; and were Browning's contributions to the religious questionings that were then perplexing men's minds. His word was, as might have been expected, emphatically on the side of faith. I have not yet mentioned that Browning's parents were Dissenters, and Dissenters of a very marked type. The poet himself was, of course, brought up in this school ; and for some years after his return from Florence attended a Congregational Chapel in Camden Town,— which was under the charge of the "poet preacher," the Rev. Thomas Jones, whose teaching was essentially that of the broad school ; but it must not be supposed that on this matter Mr. Browning's mind ran in one groove ; for, as will be evident to the reader of *Christmas Eve,* he was catholic and large-hearted to the highest degree.

Two years after the publication of *Christmas Eve,* Mr. Edward Moxon published " Letters of Percy Bysshe Shelley, with an

Introductory Essay by Robert Browning." These letters were subsequently found to be forgeries ; and the work was speedily withdrawn from sale ; but of course the responsibility for their publication in no way concerned Mr. Browning ; neither did they throw any new light on Shelley's character or life : but they at least gave Browning the chance of writing not only on the subject of Shelley, but on the true poet, his work and aims—an essay which will always prove of. interest to the student of poetry.

It was in 1855 that Mr. Browning attained the crowning point of his literary career by the publication, in two volumes, of the series of poems entitled *Men and Women*. The various poems that make up this collection were written in London and Florence, and contain some of his finest and most mature work. In these volumes there was little that could be called obscure—although such poems as *Love in a Life* and *Life in a Love*, seem to have puzzled the ordinary reader from that day to this; but a couple of volumes containing such poems as *Saul, Andrea del Sarto, By the Firesiae*, &c., must have come as a new revelation to all readers of poetry. The second volume closed with *One Word More* — in which he addresses " E. B. B. ; " the only *direct* personal note he has permitted himself to utter. The first of these volumes contained the fine poem of the

Statue and the Bust, which seems to have been regarded by certain readers as somewhat difficult. A year or two since, Mr. Wise received a copy of an American paper, in which occurred the following queries concerning the *Statue and the Bust :*

" 1.—When, how, and where did it happen ? Browning's divine vagueness lets one gather only that the lady's husband was a Riccardi ; 2.—Who was the lady ? who the duke ? 3.— The magnificent house wherein Florence lodges her Prèfet is known to all Florentine ball-goers as the Palazzo Riccardi. It was bought by the Riccardi from the Medici in 1659. From none of its windows did the lady gaze at her more than royal lover. From what window then, if from any ? Are the statue and the bust still in their original positions ? "

On the receipt of these queries, Mr. Wise forwarded them to the poet, receiving the following characteristic note in answer :—

Jan. 8th, '87.

Dear Mr. Wise,

I have seldom met with such a strange inability to understand what seems the plainest matter possible : "ball-goers" are probably not history readers, but any guide book would confirm what is sufficiently stated in the poem : I will append a note or two, however.

1.—"This story the townsmen tell"; "when, how, and where" constitutes the subject of the poem.

2.—The lady was the wife of Riccardi, and the Duke—Ferdinand, just as the poem says.

3.—As it was built by, and inhabited by the Medici till sold, long after, to the Riccardi, —it was not from the Duke's palace, but a window in that of the Riccardi, that the lady gazed at her lover riding by. The statue is still in its place, looking at the window under which "now is the empty shrine." Can anything be clearer? My "vagueness" leaves *what* to be "gathered" when all these things are put down in black and white? Oh, "ball-goers"!

Yours very sincerely,

ROBERT BROWNING.

In the *Keepsake* for 1856, edited by Miss Power, occurs a little poem by Mr. Browning, entitled *Ben Karshook's Wisdom* (dated Rome, April 27th, 1854), which, as it has not been reprinted in any of his works, I quote here (in the exact form in which it appears in the *Keepsake*):—

I.

> "Would a man 'scape the rod?"
>   Rabbi Ben Karshook saith,
> "See that he turn to God,
>   The day before his death."

" Ay, could a man inquire,
    When it shall come !" I say.
The Rabbi's eye shoots fire—
    " Then let him turn to-day !"

II.

Quoth a young Sadducee :
    " Reader of many rolls,
Is it so certain we
    Have, as they tell us, souls ? "

" Son, there is no reply !"
    The Rabbi bit his beard :
" Certain, a soul have *I*—
    We may have none," he sneered.

Thus Karshook, the Hiram's-Hammer,
    The Right-hand Temple-column,
Taught babes in grace their grammar,
    And struck the simple, solemn.

In 1861, about an hour after daybreak on
the morning of June 29, died Elizabeth Barrett
Browning; and of Mr. Browning it may
truly be said, the "light of his life had gone
out." Soon after his wife's death, the poet
returned to England; residing for many
years at 19, Warwick Crescent, Paddington;
and for the last two or three years of his life
at 29, De Vere Gardens, Kensington.

Once again in London, Mr. Browning renewed his old friendships, and made many
new ones; but for the most part, his life from
this time onward was, in the main, a record
of ever-increasing poetical work, which he

poured forth with surprising rapidity. In 1864, was published the *Dramatis Personæ*, which contains some of his best work. For the next four years he was silent, but by no means idle—indeed, about 1868, he writes me, "I have been far from well, and oppressed by work." This latter statement was truly enough substantiated when, in November, 1868, came out the first volume of a new poem (in four volumes), entitled *The Ring and the Book*— the remaining volumes being issued in each subsequent month. It is a stupendous work, —but it crowned him "chief poet of the age."

In 1870, Mr. Browning's first sonnet was written, and it appeared some few years later in the *Pall Mall Gazette.* This fine sonnet was written at the request of Lord Dufferin, having for its subject the memorial tower which had been erected at Clandeboye, Ireland, to the memory of his mother, Helen, Countess of Gifford. It was as follows :—

Who hears of Helen's Tower, may dream perchance
  How the Greek Beauty from the Scæan Gate
  Gazed on old friends unanimous in hate,
Death-doom'd because of her fair countenance.

Hearts would leap otherwise at thy advance,
  Lady, to whom this Tower is consecrate !
  Like hers, thy face once made all eyes elate,
Yet, unlike hers, was blessed by every glance.

The Tower of Hate is outworn, far and strange.;
  A transitory shame of long ago,
  It dies into the sand from which it sprang;

But thine, Love's rock-built Tower, shalt fear no
    change:
  God's self laid stable earth's foundations so,
When all the morning stars together sang.

Mr. Browning does not, however, seem to
have taken very kindly to the sonnet as a
medium for the expression of his thought;
merely reserving this for any chance word that
might need utterance. It is noteworthy that
he has not included any of what may be
termed his " chance sonnets " in his published
work: and for that reason, it may be useful
to quote here the few that have appeared in
the Press.

Following the above, Browning's next
sonnet in rank of merit, is, I think, the one
contributed to the Shakspearian show at the
Albert Hall, entitled *The Names* :—

Shakspeare ! — to such name's sounding, what
    succeeds
  Fitly as silence ? Falter forth the spell,—
  Act follows word, the speaker knows full well,
Nor tampers with its magic more than needs.
Two names there are : That which the Hebrew reads
  With his soul only : if from lips it fell,
  Echo, back thundered by earth, heaven and hell,
Would own "Thou did'st create us ! " Nought impedes
We voice the other name, man's most of might,
  Awesomely, lovingly : let awe and love
Mutely await their working, leave to sight
  All of the issue as—below—above—
  Shakspeare's creation rises : one remove,
Though dread—this finite from that infinite.

At Venice, in the November of 1883, the

following was written for the Album of the
Committee of the Goldoni Monument :—

Goldoni,—good, gay, sunniest of souls,—
　　Glassing half Venice in that verse of thine,—
　　What though it just reflect the shade and shine
Of common life, nor render, as it rolls,
Grandeur and gloom ? Sufficient for thy shoals
　　Was Carnival : Parini's depths enshrine
　　Secrets unsuited to that opaline
Surface of things which laughs along thy scrolls.
There throng the People : how they come and go,
　　Lisp the soft language, flaunt the bright garb—see—
On Piazza, Calle, under Portico
　　And over Bridge ! Dear king of Comedy,
Be honoured ! Thou that didst love Venice so,
　　Venice, and we who love her, all love thee !

Then there was the sonnet written in 1884,
in the Album presented to Arthur Chappell :

" Enter my palace," if a prince should say—
　　" Feast with the Painters ! See, in bounteous row,
　　They range from Titian up to Angelo !"
Could we be silent at the rich survey ?
A host so kindly, in as great a way
　　Invites to banquet, substitutes, for show
　　Sound that's diviner still, and bids us know
Bach like Beethoven ; are we thankless, pray ?

Thanks, then, to Arthur Chappell,—thanks to him
　　Whose every guest henceforth not idly vaunts,
　　" Sense has received the utmost Nature grants,
My cup was filled with rapture to the brim,
　　When, night by night—ah, memory, how it haunts !—
　　Music was poured by perfect ministrants,
By Halle, Schumann, Piatti, Joachim."

There were also the sonnets "Why am I a Liberal?" published in a work issued by Messrs. Cassell and Co.; and the one to ".Rawdon Brown."

Mr. Browning wrote some memorial lines for a "window," commemorative of the Jubilee, placed in St. Margaret's Church, Westminster :

> " Fifty years' flight ! wherein should he rejoice
>   Who hailed their birth, who as they die decays ?
>   This—England echoes his attesting voice ;
>   Wondrous and well — thanks Ancient Thou of
>   days."

The last of Mr. Browning's " chance words " was the well-known lines to some remarks of Edward Fitzgerald's—certainly a well-merited castigation ; but which were now best forgotten, though we can easily understand the spirit of indignation under which the poet wrote.

In 1871, the *Cornhill Magazine* contained *Hervé Riel*, the poem being dated Croisic, Sept. 30, 1867. This was Mr. Browning's sole contribution to magazines of recent years— the £100 he received for the poem being given to the French relief fund during the war with Germany. In the same year appeared *Balaustion's Adventure ; including a Transcript from Euripides.* The record of the next few years is a busy one : 1871, *Prince Hohenstiel-Schwangau, Saviour of Society ;* 1872, *Fifine at the Fair ;* 1873, *Red Cotton Nightcap Country, or Turf and Towers;* 1875, *Aristophanes' Apology,*

being the Last Adventure of Balaustion; and
the same year, the *Inn Album.*

These poems from 1871 to 1875 are surely
a record of unwearied literary productiveness;
and truly prove the correctness of his words,
"I cannot be an idle man." They did not,
however, add very much to the fame he had
already achieved, although each poem was exceedingly characteristic of its author. But
in 1876 appeared "*Pacchiarotto, and how he
worked in Distemper: with other Poems*"—these
"other Poems" being in the nature of a return
to his earlier work, and containing such gems
as "Pisgah-Sights," "At the 'Mermaid,'"
"Appearances," "St. Martin's Summer," and
"Fears and Scruples." Regarding this latter
poem, I will quote an interesting letter from
the poet himself :—

19, Warwick Crescent, W.,

Feb. 9th, '85.

My dear Kingsland,

Another of your many proofs of kindness to me! but you are no more likely to
tire of being kind than I am of being grateful.

I think that the point I wanted to illustrate
in the poem you mention was this: Where
there is a genuine love of the "letters" and
"actions" of the invisible "friend,"—however
these may be disadvantaged by an inability to
meet the objections to their authenticity or
historical value urged by "experts" who

assume the privilege of learning over ignorance,—it would indeed be a wrong to the
wisdom and goodness of the "friend" if he
were supposed capable of overlooking the ac-
tual "love" and only considering the "ignorance" which, failing to in any degree affect
"love" is really the highest evidence that
"love," exists. So I *meant*, whether the result
be clear or no. .   . . .

Yours affectionately ever,
ROBERT BROWNING.

The *Agamemnon of Æschylus* appeared in
1877 ; and in the following year, *La Saisiaz*,
and the *Two Poets of Croisic*. In 1879, Mr.
Browning issued his *Dramatic Idylls*, and the
following year a second series under the same
title. *Jocoseria* was published in 1883; and
Ferishtah's Fancies in 1884.

It may here be well to mention that in
July, 1881, a society was formed in London
by Dr. Furnivall and Miss E. H. Hickey, for
the purpose of the study and discussion of Mr.
Browning's works. The society—called the
" Browning Society "—soon got into working
order, many admirers of the poet were at once
enrolled as members, and the study of Mr.
Browning's writings set about in earnest. Dr.
Furnivall compiled an interesting and volumi-
nous " Bibliography," while various critical
papers by those best competent to speak were
read and printed. But after all, it was felt by

not a few that what was really wanted was a selection of Mr. Browning's more popular and easily-understood poems, published at a nominal price, so as to bring them within reach of what is somewhat vaguely termed "the People." Those who were able to join a society such as this, were probably the people who had leisure and means to study for themselves ; but it was felt that there was a "general reading public" to whom some of these poems should specially appeal, and the question was—how to get at them ? This was in some measure answered by means of lectures, &c. ; while the issue by Messrs. Smith and Elder of a cheaper edition of the "Selections," greatly aided in the matter—and in this regard it is pleasant to note the cordial and friendly relations that always subsisted between Mr. Browning and his publishers.

It was towards the end of 1885 that I wrote to a leading member of this Society (a friend of Mr. Browning's) on the question as to the desirability of a "People's Edition" of the more popular poems. To my dismay, I received an intimation that my letter had been sent on to Mr. Browning—of course with the obvious intention of emphasising the need of such an edition. However this might be, I certainly was averse to my crude suggestions going to head-quarters ; so I at once wrote the Poet, explaining the matter in question. His reply is, I think, well worth quoting, as it

will show that while he was fully desirous that
his works should be brought within reach of
the "People," he had implicit confidence in
the judgment of his publishers ; and like a
wise man, prefered leaving business details to
them—who after all were the only competent
judges in the matter :

> 19, Warwick Crescent,
> *Jan. 6th*, '86.

My dear Kingsland,

I did indeed get your very kind and
considerate letter addressed to ——, and
returned it to him with every acknowledge-
ment of the interest in my books which I have
—very long now—been thoroughly acquainted
with and grateful for.

With respect to the proposed cheap volume
of selections, is it necessary to say that—so
far from being indifferent to the sympathy of
" the People,"—and careless about their limited means of laying out money on books—I
began the series of " Bells and Pomegranates,"
at the price of *sixpence* a number,—which the
publisher found it advisable to raise, if he
wished to sell at all. In this case, my publisher might say that a cheap edition of the
Selections has just been printed and stereo-
typed, at half the price of the former one, and
the sale of this, which is increasingly considerable, would be checked or stopped by yet
another venture in the way of cheapness—

which, moreover, to answer its purpose, ought to comprise the more popular if not the best pieces : and what can be said in reply ? Alas, that,—as Keats complained,—in these days, "honey can't be got without hard money!"

I wish, with all my heart, I could give the honey,—or what your good nature accepts as such,— freely and without price ; but so long as there is an intermediary to account with, I am bound to consult his advantage—in business matters—as well as my own—in a pleasant liberality which would be accountable to nobody else.

I think you do not take into account the *uses* of a book purchased at even a price above the means of "the People" to pay : after it is read—how often is it bound or simply shelved and put aside exclusively for the owner ? Are books not lent, and sold secondhand, and dirtied, and cheapened still further, till they are within the reach of, at least, many a reader who would otherwise never possess them at all—even for an hour's amusement ? But I have said my little say and may leave off.   All best wishes to you and yours for the current year and its followers ! *Do* pray, whenever you wish to gratify me, come here : you will delight my sister as well as myself. Ever, with all kind regards from us both,

Yours very truly,
ROBERT BROWNING.

Hand Hotel, Llangollen, N. Wales.
Sept 6. '86.

My dear Kingsland,

I am sure you share in our sorrow when I tell you that I am informed, by a Telegram received this morning, of the death of my beloved & dear friend, Milsand.

It took place on the 4th at Villers la Haye: we had a letter from him, dated Aug: 28, in which he spoke of his increasing weakness - which did not however in any way affect his intellect; only the body has failed him.

I know you entertained much regard for him - as I know that he was much attached to you and to all your family. I am anxious therefore that you should hear of our loss from myself, and not indirectly as you might.

With every good wish from my sister, and also from me, that you and all yours may continue to enjoy health and happiness, believe me,

Yours truly ever

Robert Browning.

It was in 1886, that Mr. Browning lost by death, one of his oldest and worthiest friends, M. Milsand, of Dijon, to whom the well-known dedication of the 1863 edition of *Sordello* was written. M. Milsand was almost the first Frenchman to recognize Mr. Browning's genius or to review his poems. As early as 1851 he wrote of him in the *Révue des deux Mondes* : " Mr. Browning belongs to the family of Milton rather than of Shakespeare. His peculiar genius is that he sees in every fact an epitome of creation. I know of no poet as capable of gathering up the religious, moral, and scientific conceptions of our time, and clothing them in poetic form." The relationship between Browning and Milsand was a very beautiful one ; and it was truly delightful to see these old and staunch friends together. When Mr. Browning heard of his friend's death, he at once wrote me the letter of which a facsimile is appended.

In 1887 came the *Parleyings with certain People of Importance in their day*, bearing the following inscription : " In Memoriam, J. Milsand, Obiit iv. Sept., mdccclxxxvi, *Absens absentem auditque videtque.*" " There's poor dear Milsand," said Browning to me one day, at his house in De Vere Gardens, pointing to his friend's portrait, painted by his son ; " he was in my mind a great deal while I was writing the *Parleyings.*" Alas, but three years were to run ere Mr. Browning was to follow his friend into the "world of light."

I have not yet mentioned the few occasions on which Mr. Browning was present at public ceremonials ; but one of these stands out more boldly than the rest, and is worthy of record from the fact that the poet himself was profoundly touched by his reception, and would often speak of it with evident gratification : I refer to the celebration of the Tercentenary of the University of Edinburgh, in 1884. It was, however, at the students' reception of the University guests that Mr. Browning achieved, perhaps, the greatest popular success of his life, and became, without any premeditation or effort, one of the heroes of the memorable festival. Concerning this interesting occasion, a correspondent of the *Times* writes :— " The students arrived early and packed themselves in their allotted space. During the hour or more of waiting they had voluntarily subjected themselves to, they were surprised and gratified to find that a neatly-dressed old gentleman, with snow-white head and beard, had from his place on the platform elected to spend the waiting hour with them. At first they assumed that the venerable visitor had made a mistake, and they laughed heartily but good-naturedly, as they thought of the disappointment that was in store for him. But by-and-by, as it was seen that the old man was genuinely interested in the impromptu preliminary proceedings, and seemed unreservedly to participate in all the innocent fun in which the students indulged, a kindlier feeling was shown towards him, and the young men seemed to find pleasure in making efforts to afford entertainment for their appreciative listener and observer on the platform. By-and-by the whisper passed from bench to bench, that the faultlessly-attired, benignant-looking, white-haired visitor and observer was no other than Robert Browning; and the students, as if ashamed of the liberties they had been taking with him, relapsed into respectful, reverent silence, until one daring admirer burst out with a loud call, 'Three cheers for Browning.' Instantly the students, springing to their feet, responded to the call with stentorian cheers; while the poet, flushing and embarrassed, yet evidently highly gratified, bowed his acknowledgments, and then turned to find a less conspicuous seat. Having selected his place of retreat, he was, however, amid the thundering plaudits of the students, conducted back to his old place, the master of ceremonies on the platform having apparently explained that all the seats were allotted, and that no guest could change his place without causing confusion. The poet, however, soon recovered his composure as the places beside him became more occupied, sometimes chatting pleasantly with the gentlemen near him, at other times keep-

ing time with his foot or hand to the students'
songs, and every now and again acknowledg-
ing with unconcealed pleasure the friendly and
affectionate cheers of his young admirers.

"All through the proceedings he continued
the leading favourite. Speeches of exceptional
interest, beauty, and power, were delivered by
Sir Stafford Northcote, Mr. Lowell, and
others ; but still the cry was for "Browning,"
and at last the poet rose to his feet. He
said :—

"'Gentlemen, the utter surprise with which
this demonstration fills me, and the embarrass-
ment consequent upon it, must be my excuse
for not attempting to do more adequately
what I am afraid would in any case be done
by me most imperfectly. I am usually accused
of my writings being unintelligible. Let me,
for once, attempt to be intelligible indeed by
saying that I feel thoroughly grateful to you
for the kindness which, not only on this
occasion, but during the last two or three
days, I have experienced. I shall consider
this to the end of my life one of the proudest
days I have spent. The recognition you have
given me and all your kindness I shall never
forget.'

"Every sentence was emphasized by hearty
cheering from the students, and Sir Stafford
Northcote, gracefully responded on the part

of the meeting : ' Mr. Browning has been good enough to say that his writings are generally misunderstood, but that must be due to his audiences. I am sure that so intelligent an audience as that which I now see before me would have done ample justice to Mr. Browning's address. But we are very much obliged to him for his presence here, and for the kind recognition which he has joined in giving you.' "

Here perhaps might be the place to weave in a few personal recollections of the poet ; but they could tell little that the world does not already know concerning him. Kindly and courteous, gentle and loving, he ever was to all with whom he came in contact. It was an experience to accompany him upstairs to his " den," as he would call the handsome and spacious study in his Kensington house,—and hear him talk, discoursing sometimes of his *Pauline* days at Richmond ; and narrating how on one occasion, walking with Wordsworth and some friends, one of the party said, " There's Browning's house over by that hill." " Call *that* a hill," exclaimed Wordsworth, " why, we only call that a *rise* in my country." Then he would show you the lock of Milton's hair, given to him and his wife by Leigh Hunt ; the books and manuscripts connected with Walter Savage Landor ; and the original " square old yellow book," with its " crumpled vellum covers," which he picked up in a " square

in Florence," the finding of which led to his
writing the *Ring and the Book*. Mr. Browning seems to have had a most retentive memory ; and he would pour out early reminiscen-
ces in abundance at times : indeed, I recollect
his remarking on one occasion that he could
call to mind many things that occurred when
he was five years old, adding—" I used to
frighten my mother with my keen memory."

Now and again Mr. Browning would recall some reminiscence of his wife, or narrate
little incidents connected with her memory.
On one occasion at Warwick Crescent, when
the conversation was ranging round the ways
of little children, he abruptly broke in : " I was
one day playing a delicate piece of Chopin's
on the piano ; and on hearing a loud noise
outside the room, hastily left off playing. Just
at that moment my little boy came in—and
my wife turned round to me, saying, half in
jest and half in earnest, ' How could you have
the heart to leave off playing when he has
come in with *three drums* to accompany you ?' "

Indeed, it was a rare and especial privilege
to be shown some of the many memorials of
Elizabeth Barrett Browning. The old poet
would unlock a drawer of the table at which
he wrote, and take out a book or a faded
paper,—while the listener would detect a wist-
ful, yearning tenderness in the voice as the poet
proceeded to explain whatever object he might
be showing you.

I remember calling on him soon after the Shah's last visit to London, and it was very amusing to hear his account of the personal communication between the Persian monarch and himself. "Are you a poet?" was the first question (in French) : "Well, people are good enough to say so," replied the poet. "Have you written much?" next queried the Shah. "A great deal too much," was the modest answer. "Will you give me one of your books?" was another question,—and, said the poet, with a comical smile, "I went out next morning to Oxford Street, and bought the two volumes of selections, prettily bound, and sent him."

For Lord Tennyson he always had a large place in his heart, and would speak of him with reverent admiration—which feeling we all know was nobly reciprocated by the Laureate. It has been so customary for critics to speak of "Mr. Browning and his great rival," that a certain order of minds might well think there was a sort of personal rivalry between them. We are therefore very grateful to one of Mr. Browning's friends, for persuading Lord Tennyson to allow the following letter to be made public, written on the eve of his eightieth birthday :

"29, De Vere-gardens, W.
Aug. 5, 1889.
My dear Tennyson,
To-morrow is your birthday—indeed,

a memorable one. Let me say I associate myself with the universal pride of our country in your glory, and in its hope that for many and many a year we may have your very self among us—secure that your poetry will be a wonder and delight to all those appointed to come after. And for my own part, let me further say, I have loved you dearly. May God bless you and yours.

At no moment from first to last of my acquaintance with your works, or friendship with yourself, have I had any other feeling, expressed or kept silent, than this which an opportunity allows me to utter—that I am and ever shall be, my dear Tennyson, admiringly and affectionately yours,

ROBERT BROWNING."

It was always a pleasure to hear Mr. Browning speak of his contemporaries in literature—for the listener could not fail to note the large-hearted generosity of the man. Of Landor, Forster, Dickens, "Barry Cornwall," and others, Mr. Browning would speak with enthusiasm ; but he always had a special word of praise for Thomas Carlyle—from whom, early in his career, he had had several kindly and encouraging letters, which are now I believe in the hands of Professor Norton, for future publication. Mr. Browning used to tell how, soon after the publication of one of his early books, he had a most cordial letter from

Carlyle, asking him to call at Chelsea. So kindly was the letter, that Mr. Browning—who looked up to Carlyle with a sort of awe—thought it must be a mistake; but he nevertheless called, and was received with the greatest kindness by the philosopher and his wife. He subsequently renewed his visits; and he would relate how Carlyle and his wife would often accompany him part of the way back, "as far as Vauxhall Bridge Road," on his homeward journey. In after life, Browning always made a point of visiting Carlyle on his birthday. Shortly before his death, the old man called at Warwick Crescent. Mr. Browning was out, but Carlyle (who was too weak to leave the carriage), left a message with Miss Browning: "Tell your brother I should like to see him once again before I die." Needless to say, the poet went over to Chelsea the next morning.

Of his personal kindness to myself, I cannot here speak—but the recollection of it will be one of the sacredest of memories. He was always the same: the hearty grasp of the hand, the face smiling a welcome, the kindly ring of the voice. Hopeful and buoyant he ever was—though latterly there would be a tinge of pathos in his utterance. "That is my room," he said to me once, as he was showing me over his new house. "I shall die there—that will be my last home." "*Here* at least," he went on, "for one may surely hope it

E

will not be the *last;*" entering his study, he
said, "By and bye I do not mean to write
quite so much as I have done—and then I
shall have more time to give to my friends." I
asked him once if he would mind writing his
name in my original edition of the *Dramatis
Personæ*; and he wrote as follows: "I had
not the pleasure of giving this book to my
friend Kingsland—but there is no one for
whom I would rather have written it, if he has
got pleasure by what it contains,—Robert
Browning."

In August, 1888, I saw him for the last time.
It seemed to me he was then ageing visibly,
despite the youthfulness and buoyancy of
manner that yet asserted itself. But the old
kindliness and cheeriness was still present—
though there was a touch of pathos in his voice
as he spoke of meeting after his holiday. "If
I live," he repeated, more than once.

A few days after this, I received from Miss
Helen Clarke, of Philadelphia, some numbers
of a magazine dealing chiefly with the writings of Mr. Browning, with a request that
I would forward them to the poet. I did so,
and a few days afterwards received what
proved to be my last letter from him:

29, De Vere Gardens, W.,

My dear Kingsland,   *Aug.* 26, '89.

I have to acknowledge your kindness

in forwarding the magazines, which have much
interested me, as I looked through them last
evening . . . . I am hurried and cannot say
more, as I would gladly do if we were not
just about to start—in a day or two at
farthest. But here or away, you must remember me ever as your affectionate friend
and well-wisher. . . . . . . Will you
thank Miss Helen Clarke emphatically for
the honour and pleasure she and her like-
minded friends have done me in the magazine
and elsewhere ? I should be grateful for the
successive numbers, if the transmission would
not cause too much trouble. With kind
regards,

> Yours sincerely,
> ROBERT BROWNING

Within a day or two of writing this letter,
Mr. Browning left England for his autumn
holiday—for the last time. He spent some
pleasant weeks at Asolo ; from thence jour-
neying to Venice, where he stayed for some
time with old friends, and subsequently with
his son at the Palazzo Rezzonico. He had
intended to return to England in time for the
publication of his new book, *Asolando ;* but
just as he was about to start, he was taken
suddenly ill with bronchial catarrh. His com-
plaint, however, developed to bronchitis with
asthma, and weakness of the heart ensued.
In spite of every care and the most attentive

nursing, the poet grew weaker, though he
suffered little save inconvenience, and ate,
slept, and digested almost as well as when in
his full vigour.   On Thursday, December
12th, however, the extreme weakness of the
heart's action was very marked, and the doc-
tors feared that unless some immediate change
for the better took place a fatal lapse would
occur before long.   The poet's last hours were
by no means unhappy or overclouded ; nay,
they were what his best friends could well
have desired for him.   He was free from pain,
and, save for his cardiac weakness, feeling
better ; was greatly cheered by the sympathy
displayed by the numerous telegrams which
he had received ; and those near and dear to
him were by his side.   He also experienced
much pleasure from the receipt of more than
one telegram telling him of the wide and immediate success of his new book *Asolando*,
which had been more largely " subscribed for "
than any of his other works.   So the day wore
on, till, about 10 o'clock in the evening, the
great poet painlessly entered Life.

It was decided to remove the poet's remains
from the Palazzo Rezzonico to the island
cemetery at Venice, as a temporary resting-
place.   A short service having been held in
the palace, the body was placed in a gondola,
bearing at the prow the figure of an angel, at
the stern that of a lion,—" he, with voice

of angel, heart of lion, lay between the two,"—
and covered with lovely flowers, many of them
sent from Florence. The relatives and friends,
and members of the Venetian Syndic, followed
in other gondolas, and so, in the light of the
setting sun, the mournful but picturesque procession moved slowly across the lagoons of
the city which the dead poet has immortal-
ised in his verse, " where the Doges used to
wed the sea with rings, where St. Mark's is,"
to the island of San Michele, where the body
was placed in the chapel.

It had been the poet's wish to be laid in the
same grave with his wife in the old cemetery
at Florence ; and application was at once made
to the proper authorities there. It was however
found to be impossible to re-open the cemetery
without an Act of Parliament ; and under these
circumstances, Mr. Barrett Browning, the
poet's son, acquiesced (in accordance with
the earnest wishes of many of the deceased
poet's contemporaries and friends) in the desire
of the Dean Bradley, that the remains of his
father should be interred in Westminster
Abbey, and the body was therefore subsequently removed from Venice to De Vere
Gardens, London.

On the last day of December, 1889, at noon,
all that was mortal of Robert Browning was
laid in the Abbey of Westminster, his grave
being fittingly found in Poet's Corner, close to
spot where lie the remains of Dryden, Chau-

cer, and Cowley. Over London, there had
floated all the morning a thick fog, but the
Abbey was, nevertheless, thronged with
mourners. Art, science, and literature, were
represented ; men and women were present
who had become the nobler and stronger
through the inspiration of his verse ; while in
that part of the edifice open unrestricted to the
public could be seen a vast crowd, composed
mostly of young men and young women, drawn
there out of love to the great poet, who was, to
use his own expressive words, "greater than
the world suspects." Strangely suggestive to
many who had known and loved the poet was
the sudden lifting of the fog soon after noon,
just at the time when the music of Croft and
Purcell was borne to the ears of the vast congregation. The clergy of the Abbey, on the
arrival of the body, formed in procession and
walked from the altar to the door of the west
cloister, and returned with the bearers of the
coffin ; the officiating clergy were the Dean,
the Sub-Dean (Canon Prothero), Canon
Duckworth, Canon Furse, and Dr. Troutbeck
(precentor). Slowly the sad procession passed
within the choir, and the bearers bore the
coffin, covered with a purple pall, to the open
space assigned to it—the pall-bearers being :
Mr. Hallam Tennyson, representing the Poet
Laureate, Sir James Fitzjames Stephen, the
Master of Trinity, Sir Theodore Martin, Arch-
deacon Farrar, the Master of Balliol, Professor

Masson, Sir Frederick Leighton, Sir James
Paget, Sir G. Grove, Professor Knight, and
Mr. George Smith. By the side of the Dean
of Westminster at the bottom of the choir
were the Archbishop of Canterbury, and Capt.
Walter Campbell, the latter representing the
Queen. Upon the top of the coffin were some
exquisite wreaths, one of white immortelles ;
another of violets and lilies of the valley, and
a massive cross of violets. The service began
with the chanting of the 90th Psalm, " Lord,
Thou hast been our refuge," to Purcell's music,
and then Canon Prothero read the appointed
lesson. Next followed the beautiful words of
Mrs. Browning, to which Dr. Bridge had composed a musical setting of the tenderest pathos,
and in full harmony with the thought of the
poem. Very sacred was it to listen to these
words of the wife who had been taken from her
husband some eight-and-twenty years before,
but had left him a legacy of love as rare as it
was beautiful :

What would we give to our beloved ?
The hero's heart to be unmoved,
 The poet's star-tuned harp to sweep,
The patriot's voice to teach and rouse,
The monarch's crown to light the brows ?—
 " He giveth His belovèd sleep."

O earth, so full of dreary noises !
O men, with wailing in your voices !
 O delved gold, the wailers heap !

O strife, O curse, that o'er it fall !
God strikes a silence through you all,
　　And "giveth His belovèd sleep."

His dews drop mutely on the hill,
His cloud above it saileth still,
　　Though on its slopes men sow and reap ;
More softly than the dew is shed,
Or cloud is floated overhead,
　　" He giveth His belovèd sleep."

Following this came Wesley's anthem,
"All go to one place" (Eccles. iii. 20), and
then the clergy, the pall-bearers, and the
mourners moved after the coffin towards the
spot where the grave had been prepared.

The coffin having been lowered into the
grave, the choral part of the service for the
burial of the dead was sung. Around the
grave, with the clergy and pall-bearers, stood
the sorrowing friends and relatives of the great
poet who had passed into the Unseen ; while
the Dean pronounced the committal to the
earth, and read the prayer and collect. Then
came a burst of music from the organ, and the
whole of the vast congregation, rising, joined
the choir in singing the well-known hymn :

"O God our help in ages past,
　　Our hope for years to come ;
　Our shelter from the stormy blast,
　　And our eternal home."

Very solemn and affecting was the singing

of these words, and it will not soon be forgotten by those who heard it; many of the audience were deeply moved, and even the most indifferent spectator (had such an one been present) must have felt something of the high and holy spirit which seemed to fill the place, and which had animated the great and good man now being laid to his rest. Standing by the open grave, on that dim December afternoon, while the strains of Watts' noble hymn were surging through the old Abbey, there came forcibly to mind the resonant line from *La Saisiaz*:

" He at least believed in *soul*—was *very sure* of God."

And that other far-reaching line from the earlier poem of *Saul:*

" It shall be
A Face like my face that receives thee ; a Man like to
     me,
Thou shalt love and be loved by for ever : a Hand
     like to my hand
Shall throw open the gates of new life to thee—see the
     Christ stand ! "

The gates have been opened for Robert Browning—he has seen *all :* he has realised his own words in *Prospice :*

" O thou soul of my soul, I shall see thee again,
     And with God be the rest."

The Benediction, followed by the Dead

·March, brought this sad and impressive service to a close.

"And I heard a voice from Heaven, saying: Blessed are the dead which die in the Lord; yea, saith the Spirit, for they rest from their labours, and their works do follow them."

" Death is swallowed up in victory:

"Thanks be to God which giveth us the victory through our Lord Jesus Christ."

II.

I HAVE already noted that the anonymous publication of Mr. Browning's first poem, *Pauline*, in 1833, attracted but little attention, yet a few highly-gifted spirits saw in it the sure indications of genius, and prophesied of its author yet greater things. As the years went by, these prophesies were more than realised, but though many readers of poetry fought rather shy of each succeeding volume, the "select few," soon after the publication of *Paracelsus*, recognized that once more a giant had appeared upon the earth, and welcomed each new poem with a fervour and a heartiness which must have more than compensated its author for the neglect of the general reading public.

On the publication of the *Ring and the Book*, however, in 1868 and 1869, the public could hold out no longer, and fascinated by the wealth of imagery and of thought, as by the dramatic vividness of the narrative, were constrained to hail Robert Browning as one of the chief singers of the day.

At the same time, there remained a large class of intelligent people who were repelled by what they called the "obscure style," the "harsh and involved expressions," the "ambiguity" of this most incisive and vigorous of modern poets. Some critics, indeed, went so far as to affirm that the "obscurity" was wilful; and that the poet had seen fit, for some occult reason of own, to "puzzle" his readers. This theory has long since exploded, and indeed could never have been tenable; as will be seen by a letter written by Mr. Browning upwards of twenty years ago, an extract from which has already been made public:

19, Warwick Crescent, W.
Nov. 27, '68.

My dear Mr. Kingsland,
　　Will the kindness that induced you to write your very gratifying letter forgive the delay that has taken place in answering it?—an unavoidable delay, for I have been far from well, and oppressed by work.

I am heartily glad I have your sympathy for what I write: intelligence, by itself, is scarcely the thing with respect to a new book, —as Wordsworth says (a little altered) "you must like it before it be worthy of your liking." In spite of your intelligence and sympathy, I can have little doubt but that my writing has been, in the main, too hard for many I should have been pleased to communicate with: but I never designedly tried to puzzle people, as some of my critics have supposed. On the other hand, I never pretended to offer such literature as should be a substitute for a cigar, or game at dominos to an idle man. So perhaps on the whole I get my deserts and something over,—not a crowd but a few I value more. Let me remember gratefully that I may class you among these : while you, in turn, must remember me as,

Yours very faithfully,
ROBERT BROWNING.

But unfortunately, in spite of Mr. Browning's asseverations that he has never been " wilfully obscure," many readers of poetry still incline to the belief that in some way or other it is *his* fault if they fail to catch his meaning ; and after one or two futile attempts at some poem utterly beyond them at that stage of their reading, give up the thing altogether. Thus it comes about that Mr. Browning's poems have been neglected by many who might otherwise have felt drawn to them, and it is with the hope of interesting readers of this class that this book has been written.

It may be well to note, first, some of the main characteristics of Browning's work ; and it must be stated at the outset, that he is emphatically the poet of Faith and Hope,— the truly religious poet. At the same time, he is a man of the world, with a large knowledge of men and things, and an altogether marvellous insight into human nature.

Great, indeed, is the range of his genius, and

universal the sources of his inspiration. Popes,
monks, saints, kings, queens, children, villains,
throng his canvas, and from one and all some
deep human experience is evolved. In *Pippa
Passes*—perhaps the most beautiful, as it .is
probably the most easily comprehended of his
dramas—he gives us a charming picture of
Pippa, a little factory girl, who, moving anear
to souls soiled by evil in her one day's holiday,
sings her little snatches of song like the lark
at heaven's gate, awaking dead conscience and
remorse in hard, bad hearts, instancing once
more the power of the old-world words, " out
of the mouth of babes and sucklings Thou hast
perfected praise : " and the burden of whose
song, as she descends like a child-angel into
the light of a new morning, with the spring-
world bathed in the glory and gold of a blessed
sunrise, is

> " The year 's at the spring,
> And day 's at the morn ;
> Morning 's at seven ;
> The hill-side 's dew-pearled,
> The lark 's on the wing ;
> The snail 's on the thorn ;
> God 's in His Heaven—
> All 's right with the world."

The range of Mr. Browning's genius is
as unique as it is catholic. Are you fond of
thought cast in a dramatic mould ? Then you
can have your choice amid half a dozen of the
ripest dramas of the last fifty years—dramas

that reach even the "high-water mark" of the dramatists of the Elizabethan period— beginning with *Strafford* and ending with *Luria.* Does Art appeal to you? Then you have some pregnant teaching on painting and sculpture in *Old Pictures in Florence, Fra Lippo,* and *Andrea del Sarto.* Do you love to peer into the recesses of the human heart, and probe to the utmost motive and conscience? Then must you go to Browning, and the *Ring and the Book,* and the *Dramatic Idylls,* will furnish you with an ever-widening series of studies on conscience and mental analysis. Does music speak to you? Here you will find not only perfect poems, but the ripest thought on music to be found in modern literature— poems which culminate in the rapt vision of *Abt Vogler.* Lastly—are you moved by the religious questionings of the age? Are you profoundly touched by religious thought? Then here is your poet ready to hand; and in *Saul,* onward to the *Death in the Desert, Ferishtah's Fancies,* and *Asolando,* you will will find the ripened wisdom of a religious teacher whose teachings transcend theology, and the key-note of whose belief is

I say, the acknowledgment of God in Christ,
Accepted by thy reason, solves for thee
All questions in the earth and out of it,
And has so far advanced thee to be wise.
"Death in the Desert."

In a word, Mr. Browning is pre-eminently *the*
religious poet—healthy, manly, brave; with a
hope like Jacob's ladder, reaching from earth
to the highest heaven. To him, Hope is visible the world round. He walks one day
through Paris streets and steps into the Morgue,
where the corpses of suicides were wont
to be ranged for the public gaze. And there
lay three specimens of humanity,

> "Poor men, God made, and all for that !
>   The reverence struck me ; o'er each head
> Religiously was hung its hat,
>   Each coat dripped by the owner's bed,
> Sacred from touch : each had his berth,
>   His bounds, his proper place of rest,
> Who last night tenanted on earth
>   Some arch, where twelve such slept abreast—
> Unless the plain asphalte seemed best."

The poet then proceeds to read the secret of
each heart, probing with his keen analytical
power the secret of the life thrown away, and
finding the source of despair that induced self
destruction:

> "How did it happen, my poor boy ?
>   You wanted to be Buonaparte
> And have the Tuileries for toy,
>   And could not, so it broke your heart ?
> You, old one by his side, I judge,
>   Were, red as blood, a socialist,
> A leveller ! Does the Empire grudge
>   You've gained what no Republic missed ?
> Be quiet, and unclench your fist !

> "And this—why he was red in vain,
>   Or black—poor fellow that is blue !
> What fancy was it turned your brain ?
>   Oh, women were the prize for you !
> Money gets women, cards and dice
>   Get money, and ill-luck gets just
> The copper couch and one clear nice
>   Cool squirt of water o'er your bust,
> The right thing to extinguish lust ! "

Note the indignant burst of these last lines !
Browning has only contempt for mere sensu-
ality—as, indeed, what else could such a man
have ?   So, gazing on these corpses, thinking
of the sin and wretchedness that lured a human soul to a self-sought death, he exclaims :

> " I thought, and think their sin 's atoned."

Following with that strong, optimistic stanza,
in which he expresses his belief that evil is not
eternal ;   that God lives, therefore Hope is
assured ; and that the destruction of one human
soul is alien to the character of the Maker :

> " It 's wiser being good than bad ;
>   It 's safer being meek than fierce :
> It 's fitter being sane than mad.
>   My own hope is, a sun will pierce
> The thickest cloud earth ever stretched ;
>   That, after Last, returns the First,
> Though a wide compass round be fetched ;
>   That what began best, can't end worst,
> Nor what God blessed once, prove accurst."

F

III.

BEFORE, however, we go any further in our brief study of the leading characteristics of Mr. Browning's work, we must lay stress upon the fact that he is, first and foremost, a *poet*. What is a poet? What do we mean when we call a man a "chief singer," when we claim for him the title of *poet*? Primarily he must be a *teacher*; he must have a message to deliver, a doctrine to propound; and he must assuredly be a *thinker*. But still all this would not constitute him a poet. There is an undefinable something else wanting. He must combine with these qualities the rare power of giving utterance to his thoughts in words that shall thrill the imagination; his lines must be rainbow-coloured, as it were; they must be blended with a fancy, wedded to a music, that shall sing themselves into the mind of the reader. He who has this gift *is* a poet—he who has it not, may be a clever and pleasing versifier, but is no poet.

Now I hold that Robert Browning possessed in a large measure this superb and unique gift. Had he not felt *impelled* to poetry, undoubtedly he would have turned his genius into another channel: but he could not help

being a poet—his words naturally form themselves into musical rhythm ; his sentences are
coloured as with the brush of a Turner; and
throb with life, like a summer morning.   But
then, Mr. Browning's thoughts come so fast,
they flow forth in such rich and prodigal pro-
fusion, that they as often as not hide the exquisite play of fancy, the sweet musical ripple,
that lies beneath them.   And so one sometimes has to search deep for the jewel—to read
and re-read ; and, unfortunately, this is just
what many modern readers cannot be persuaded to do.   Thereupon they say, as was
said from the time of *Sordello*, "We cannot
understand this Browning—*we* cannot find the
golden nugget you tell us is there, so we give
it up."   Thus has our poet been termed un-
popular, obscure, devoid of music, and so on.
Now a very little patience on the reader's part
would have altered all this ; and by a second
or third reading, he would not only have found
beneath the poet's world of words a vein of
rich ore, but have discovered that he was in an
altogether new country, the strange beauty of
which would have fascinated his mind and
gladdened his heart.

Having said this much, however, it must at
the same time be confessed that the poet is
often apparently indifferent to mere form or
beauty of expression.   In some of his later
poems especially, there is at times a rugged-
ness which would tend to repel the beginner ;

while the twists and turns of his sentences, and the involved grammar, *does* at times hinder one's enjoyment of his work. Often his expression appears to a novice exceedingly "odd," though startling and forceful ; and the dramatic style he has so largely adopted in telling a story, and which often seems to presuppose knowledge on the reader's part of what has gone before, when combined with this involved form of writing, does certainly render the thought exceedingly difficult to follow. That he *could* be, and often *is*, musical in the highest degree I am now endeavouring to prove ; but that he was at times really careless as to mere beauty of expression, is to be duly acknowledged and regretted.

Browning has been, and most truly, ranked with Shakspeare in the quality of his genius ; he has all Shakspeare's catholicity, his breadth of vision, his insight into human nature ; at the same time, it has always seemed to me that there is a great deal in Browning akin to Shelley. It will readily be conceded that Shelley has the greatest *lyric* gift of all English poets,—that he is, indeed, our foremost *singer ;* his poems read like melodies heard in the twilight ; like the music of the wind sweeping amid the trees of the forest, like the lullaby of the ocean waves ; and I believe that Browning possesses this gift in an almost equal degree with Shelley, but that, owing to his superabundant thought, he has

used it less, or where it is oftenest used, it is
as often hidden by the massiveness of the
message he has to deliver. In deep spiritual
experience and mental power (as for instance,
in *Saul*), he rises far above Shelley ; and it
is this very wealth of mind that sometimes
causes an apparent obscurity and overweighs
the music of his verse. In Browning's earlier
work, the *poetry* comes more into play, his
fancy seems more jubilant, his pictures more
delicately-coloured : take this, for instance,
from his first work, *Pauline* :

Thou wilt remember one warm morn, when winter
Crept aged from the earth, and Spring's first breath
Blew soft from the moist hills ; the black-thorn
    boughs,
So dark in the bare wood, when glistening
In the sunshine were white with coming buds,
Like the bright side of a sorrow, and the banks
Had violets opening from sleep like eyes.

Or from the same poem :

This is the very heart of the woods, all round
Mountain-like heaped above us ; yet even here
One pond of water gleams ; far off the river
Sweeps like a sea, barred out from land ; but one—
One thin, clear sheet has over-leaped and wound
Into this silent depth, which gained, it lies
Still, as but let by suffrance ; further on,
Tall rushes and thick flag-knots have combined
To narrow it ; so, at length, a silver thread,
It winds, all noiselessly through the deep wood,
Till, thro' a cleft-way, thro' the moss and stone,
It joins its parent-river with a shout !

But if Mr. Browning has written one work in which his poetic colouring and wealth of imagination is most superb, that work is *Sordello.* Long before I learned to love or understand this poém, I had found out its poetic wealth, and had culled from it sentence after sentence of jewel-like thoughts that were scattered through its pages thick as daisies in a spring meadow. It is a veritable storehouse for the poet ; there is hardly a page which does not radiate with poetic simile or lurid word-painting ; and one may, without exaggeration, speak of *Sordello* as one of the *richest* poems in the language. It is a very easy thing for any one to take up this poem, pick out a page at random, read it aloud, and then triumphantly ask what it all means: it is doubtless a hard task to faithfully persevere in one's first reading of the poem. It *is* difficult ; there is no doubt about that ; but, as the poet himself has said, "with care for a man or a book" many difficulties can be overcome. The faithful student, who persistently sets himself down to its study, going over its pages not once but many times, will be amply rewarded. The poem is full of spiritual teaching ; it will enlarge his knowledge; deepen his reverence ; and impress his understanding ; he will find it a real contribution to our human experience ; full of wise thoughts ; and containing pearls of rare and exceeding value. To show what I mean by the richness of the poetic mine in

Sordello, I take a few extracts at random from its pages :—

> " That autumn eve was stilled :
> A last remains of sunset dimly burned
> O'er the far forests, like a torch-flame turned
> By the wind back upon its bearer's hand
> In one long flare of crimson ; as a brand,
> The woods beneath lay black."

> " Dante, pacer of the shore
> Where glutted hell disgorgeth filthiest gloom,
> Unbitten by its whirring sulphur-spume—
> Or whence the grieved and obscure waters slope
> Into a darkness quieted by hope ;
> Plucker of amaranths grown beneath God's eye
> In gracious twilights where His chosen lie."

> " Shrinking Caryatides
> Of just-tinged marble like Eve's lilied flesh
> Beneath her Maker's finger when the fresh
> First pulse of life shot brightening the snow."

> " The breezy morning fresh
> Above, and merry,—all his waving mesh
> Laughing with lucid dew-drops rainbow-edged."

> " Songs go up exulting, then dispread,
> Dispart, disperse, lingering overhead
> Like an escape of angels."

> " A footfall there
> Suffices to upturn to the warm air
> Half-germinating spices ; mere decay
> Produces richer life."

> " Her head that's sharp and perfect like a pear
> So close and fine are laid the few fine locks
> Coloured like honey oozed from topmost rocks
> Sun-blanched the live-long summer."

In *Pippa Passes*, the reader will find a stanza
which Turner alone, perhaps, could have put
upon canvas—so rich and profuse is its colouring ; while the inspiration of the poet seems
to outsoar his capacity of writing down his
words ere they vanish in a whirl of rainbow-
coloured mist. It is a description of daybreak, and forms the opening to the poem :—

Day !
Faster and more fast,
O'er night's brim, day boils at last ;
Boils, pure gold, o'er the cloud-cup's brim
Where spurting and suppressed it lay ;
For not a froth-flake touched the rim
Of yonder gap in the solid gray
Of the eastern cloud, an hour away ;
But forth one wavelet, then another, curled,
Till the whole sunrise, not to be suppressed,
Rose, reddened, and its seething breast
Flickered in bounds, grew gold, then overflowed the
    world.

And such things are scattered throughout the
whole of Browning's pages ; we have but
glanced at a few of them floating on the surface. The true lover of English poetry will
not be content with glancing, but will dive
deeply after these pearls of thought and har-
monies of language, and will make them his
own ; he will be the richer and gladder all his
days for their possession ; and will never regret
that, undeterred by their apparent difficulty,
" he sought till he found."

In Mr. Browning's first acknowledged work, *Paracelsus,* will be found many such gems. It contains much of his highest teaching, and is a poem which once read, must be re-read and pondered over: is as fresh to-day as it was a fresh revelation to the lovers of poetry fifty years ago ; and is to be read as much for its music as for its wealth of thought. Take this passage, for example:

" Friends," I would say, " I went far, far for them,
Past the high rocks the haunt of doves, the mounds
Of red earth from whose sides strange trees grow out,
Past tracts of milk-white minute blinding sand,
Till, by a mighty moon, I tremblingly
Gathered these magic herbs, berry and bud,
In haste, not pausing to reject the weeds,
But happy plucking them at any price.
To me, who have seen them bloom in their own soil,
They are scarce lovely : plait and wear them, you !
And guess, from what they are, the springs that fed
    them,
The stars that sparkled o'er them, night by night,
The snakes that travelled far to sip their dew !"

Again, see the play of fancy—the poet-heart —in such passages as these :—

"As one spring wind unbinds the mountain snow
And comforts violets in their hermitage."

            " Though dark and drear
Appears the world before us, we no less
Wake with our wrists and ankles jewelled still."

            " A light
Will struggle through these thronging words at last,
As in the angry and tumultuous West
A soft star trembles through the drifting clouds."

"God is the perfect poet,
Who in his person acts his own creations."

"Are there not
Two points in the adventure of the diver,
One,—when, a beggar, he prepares to plunge,
One,—when, a prince, he rises with his pearl?"

"And she is gone; sweet human love is gone.
'Tis only when they spring to heaven that angels
Reveal themselves to you; they sit all day
Beside you, and lie down at night by you
Who care not for their presence, muse or sleep,
And all at once they leave you, and you know them."

Here, again, is a truly magnificent passage
from the same poem—unequalled in its de-
scriptive and imaginative power, so far as my
reading extends, by any English poet—at
least of the modern school. Have those who
so often decry the *poetic* power of Browning
ever read this passage? It reveals to the utmost the daring imagination and "fulness" of
the poet's vision; and, remembering the then
age of the writer (22), is mavellous in its realistic force:—

The centre-fire heaves underneath the earth,
And the earth changes like a human face;
The molten ore bursts up among the rocks,
Winds into the stone's heart, outbranches bright
In hidden mines, spots barren river-beds,
Crumbles into fine sand where sunbeams bask—
God joys therein. The wroth sea's waves are edged
With foam, white as the bitten lip of hate,
When, in the solitary waste, strange groups
Of young volcanos come up, cyclops-like,

Staring together with their eyes on flame—
God tastes a pleasure in their uncouth pride,
Then all is still; earth is a wintry clod:
But spring-wind, like a dancing psaltress, passes
Over its breast to waken it, rare verdure
Buds tenderly upon rough banks, between
The withered tree-roots and the cracks of frost,
Like a smile striving with a wrinkled face;
The grass grows bright, the boughs are swoln with
　　blooms
Like chrysalids impatient for the air,
The shining dorrs are busy, bettles run
Along the furrows, ants make their ado;
Above, birds fly in merry flocks, the lark
Soars up and up, shivering for very joy;
Afar the ocean sleeps; white fishing-gulls
Flit where the strand is purple with its tribe
Of nested limpets; savage creatures seek
Their loves in wood and plain—and God renews
His ancient rapture. Thus he dwells in all,
From life's minute beginnings, up at last
To man.

To those, however, who look on poetry simply as an amusement, Mr. Browning has nothing to say. The true poet he believes is a seer, bringing a veritable God's message to us; what is it but this fact that gives the best poetry so soothing and religious an effect on our minds? Hear Mrs. Browning in her *Aurora Leigh:*

"I write
Of the only truth-tellers now left to God,
The only speakers of essential truth,
The only teachers who instruct mankind. . .
. . . And while your common men
Lay telegraphs, gauge railroads, reign, reap, dine

And dust the flaunty carpets of the world,
For kings to walk on, or our president,
The poet suddenly will catch them up,
With his voice like a thunder—" This is soul,
This is life, this word is being said in heaven,
Here 's God down on us ! what are you about ? "

Now this is what Browning does for us. He reveals to us, far above the storm-clouds of this lower world, the unsoiled blue of the heavens; we can gaze with him upon the fair earth, upon the sunset sky, upon the human hearts to which ours are knit in bonds of eternal love—and find the root and origin of all in an eternal Father. Ever, as in the Seer's vision of old, do the angels ascend and descend ; ever are the heavens one with the earth—one in the wide brotherhood of the race.

IV.

BROWNING is one of the healthiest of modern English poets; there is nothing morbid in his writing,—as he himself so recently told us : of necessity, therefore, he takes an intensely earnest view of Life and its duties. To him this present life is not the play time, but the apprenticeship of the soul ; not the place for rest, but for good, honest, hearty work :

> " Life is probation, and this earth no goal
> But starting point of man."

For him there can be no eventual failure ; there may be, often, an apparent failure—the soul may be " unmade " by folly, unmanned by evil ; but the nobler part of man's nature must finally triumph—and the soul will be *remade* in those " other heights in other lives," which shall yet be a reality to every son of Adam. If a man does fail in his pursuit after Truth, or Goodness, or Beauty, he is not finally overcome ; he has gained somewhat—he has *endeavoured ;* for, had he not *attempted* he could not have failed ; consequently, failure but implies ultimate success.

Taking the completed round of his work

from *Paracelsus*, to *Asolando*, the reader
will find that Mr. Browning is essentially optimistic. To him, life is a glad, sweet thing, so
he will rejoice therein, and be glad ; he does
not, as did Byron, bemoan his condition,
"open his breast" to gain praise and pity ;
preach on the vanity of life, and then endeavour to recruit his faded energies by sen-
sual pleasure. By no means : life *is* a serious
and earnest piece of business, there is not
doubt about *that*—yet it is also a beautiful and
joyous thing withal, and to be enjoyed as the
Giver meant it to be. Look at the hearty
robustness of these verses, and ponder well on
the answer the poet gives to each question
he asks :

> " Have you found your life distasteful ?
>   My life did and does smack sweet.
> Was your youth of pleasure wasteful ?
>   Mine I saved and hold complete.
> Do your joys with age diminish ?
>   When mine fail me, I'll complain.
> Must in death your daylight finish ?
>   My sun sets to rise again.

> " What, like you, he proved—your Pilgrim—
>   This our world, a wilderness ;
> Earth still gray and heaven still grim,
>   Not a hand there his might press,
> Not a heart his own might throb to,
>   Men all rogues, and women—say
> Dolls which boys' heads duck and bob to,
>   Grown folks drop or throw away ?

" My experience being other,
   How should I contribute verse
Worthy of your king and brother ?
   Balaam-like I bless, not curse.
I find earth not gray but rosy,
   Heaven not grim but fair of hue,
Do I stoop ? I pluck a posy.
   Do I stand and stare ? All's blue."

This is Browning's central creed, round which all his thought revolves—the preciousness of *striving*, and the consequent growth of the soul. In Attainment here, says the poet, a man has gained the world, but lost his soul : once let him say that he *has* attained —what more has he to live for ? it is the *struggle* that makes life worth living, the continued *endeavour*, the seeking after Attainment. In his Art poems especially, Mr. Browning teaches that the true glory of Art, of whatever kind, consists in this—from its inception in the mind of the worker, onward to its outer manifestation, there ever comes to the artist who works for Art's sake, desires and aspirations which reach *beyond* his art— culminating in Eternity. Any artist, be he brain-worker or hand-worker, who avers that he can, in this limited life, realize his highest ideal, has *failed*—for the search after the highest is a continued endeavour ; there is a perfection even beyond perfection : the highest on earth implies a Higher in Heaven. So the true worker is he who, through repeated failures, through all unsatisfied longings and unfulfilled aspirations, reaches upward to God :

> " Ah, but a man's reach should exceed his grasp,
>   Or what 's a heaven for ? "

The reader will find much of Mr. Browning's chief utterances on this subject in *Old Pictures in Florence*, where the poet avers that the art of ancient Greece was a failure, inasmuch as it was finite; while the real greatness of early Christian art consisted in its incompleteness—nay, in its very faults; these latter leading to aspiration and endeavour.

> " For time theirs—ours for eternity."

The same idea also being emphasised in *Saul* :

> " 'Tis not what man Does which exalts him, but what
>   man Would do."

Perhaps the noblest ode we have on life and its duties is to be found in Browning's *Rabbi Ben Ezra*. It is a poem one should know by heart; it has lines in it that chant themselves into our understanding ; and its wise, weighty, and cheerful words should be a comfort under all circumstances of life.   Much of Browning's theory of life is to be found in this poem.   Take this, for example :

> " Then, welcome each rebuff
> That turns earth's smoothness rough,
> Each sting that bids nor sit nor stand but go !

Be our joys three-parts pain !
Strive, and hold cheap the strain ;
Learn, nor account the pang ; dare, never grudge the
    throe !

As it was better, youth
Should strive, through acts uncouth,
Toward making, than repose on aught found made :
So, better, age, exempt
From strife, should know, than tempt
Further. Thou waitest age ; wait death nor be afraid.

But I need, now as then
Thee, God, who mouldest men !

  .   .   .   .

My times be in Thy hand !
Perfect the cup as planned !
Let age approve of youth, and death complete the
    same !"

Take, too, these lines from *Parleyings*, and
see how well they fit in with the teaching of
his earlier work—how glad their faith, how
noble their sense of triumph :

" What if the rose-streak of morning,
Pale and depart in a passion of tears?
Once to have hoped is no matter for scorning !
Love once—e'en love's disappointment endears !
A minute's success pays the failure of years.

Age ? Why, fear ends there : the contest concluded,
Man *did* live his life, *did* escape from the fray ;
Not scratchless, but unscathed, he somehow eluded
Each blow fortune dealt him, and conquers to-day :
To-morrow—new chance and fresh strength—might we
    say ?
Laud then Man's life—no defeat but a triumph !"

                           G

V.

I HAVE said that Browning is a religious poet
—that his mind is permeated by the Christian story. It is a grand thing that a man
like Browning, with so supreme an intellect,
should be a man of firm religious belief. At
73 years of age, he produced *Ferishtah's
Fancies*, in which he reiterated his belief in
God, in the efficacy of prayer, and in immortality; and five years later came *Asolando*,
with the same hopeful and triumphant message. As to the personal religious belief
of Mr. Browning we have no right to
hazard a question, indeed, there is far too
much, now-a-days, of this curious inquiry into
the private life of our great teachers; from
a man's life-work alone are we at liberty to
gather what we may of the tendency of his
mind and the workings of his soul; and it is
from his work alone that we can judge him.
But such a man as Robert Browning could
not fail to put some of his deepest convictions upon art and life into the mouths
of many of his imaginary "men and women,"
and from these, without impertinence, we may
learn something of the spiritual truths that
were evidently part and parcel of the poet's life.

Undoubtedly, the noblest religious poems in English literature, are *Christmas-Eve and Easter-Day, Saul,* and the *Death in the Desert ;* and these are the poems in which the specially religious thought of Mr. Browning is manifest. In them he stands forth as the champion of the Christian faith—not the champion of orthodoxy, but of Christianity. The great strength of Browning, as a leader of thought in the nineteenth century, lies, to a large extent, in his acceptance of the Christian faith—not, be it understood, his acceptance of the doctrines of any school of theology, or in adherence to any dogmatic creed, for he is too great to be bandied about by any theological school—but in his acceptance of the Divine Man, "who came and dwelt on earth awhile," as the source of all that is good and great in human nature, and as the Regenerator of the race.

Browning's poem of *La Saisiaz* is often mentioned as evidence of the poet's Theistic views ; and the statement has been advanced by some of the Agnostic school that for some years preceding his death he had left the sunny ways of *Saul, Christmas Eve, Death in the Desert,* and *Prospice,* for the colder regions of theistical speculation. I cannot accept this ; it is true, the name of Christ does not appear in the poem, but the *spirit* of Christ is there, and the triumphant ring of faith at the close very firm :

' He at least believed in soul ; was *very sure* of God."

How could he be sure of God unless he
knew Christ ? "I in the Father, and the Father in me." "He that hath seen me, hath
seen the Father." If he simply thought of
(not believed in) God, as a mere cold abstraction—a sort of gaseous ether " floating in the
wide bosom of the All "—then he might call
himself a Theist ; but surely would have no
trust in immortality, which, if he believes in
soul, he must have. But nowhere do we find
Browning speaking of God in the sense of a
mere abstraction ; he does speak of Him as a
personality ; as one to whom he can utterly and
fearlessly commit himself, as, in fact, a Father
—and " the Father" implies the lover, the
friend, the brother, the fulness of whose Fa-
therhood was revealed by the Christ :

"So the All great were the All loving too."

Nor would the mere belief in the existence
of a God warrant his belief in the eternity
of love, as implied, for instance, in the poems
of *Any Wife to any Husband*, and *Evelyn
Hope*. But a belief in Christ, as the Divine and
Eternal Love, would warrant it.
Again, in *Rabbi Ben Ezra*, we have the
same idea.

> "Praise be Thine !
> I see the whole design,
> I, who saw Power, see now Love perfect too : .

> Perfect I call Thy plan :
> Thanks that I was a man !
> Maker, remake, complete,—I trust what Thou
>   shalt do !"

Twenty-five years later, the same thought is confirmed ; the poet has now reached extreme old age, but the Power—God—is still as evident to his mind : but no less evident is *Love. The Reverie* (in *Asolando*) confirms and strengthens *Rabbi Ben Ezra :*

> " Then life is—to wake not sleep,
>   Rise and not rest, but press
> From earth's level where blindly creep
>   Things perfected, more or less,
> To the heaven's height, far and steep,
>
> " Where, amid what strifes and storms
>   May await the adventurous quest,
> *Power is love*—transports, transforms
>   Who aspired from worst to best,
> Sought the soul's world, spurned the worms'.
>
> " I have faith such end shall be :
>   *From the first, Power was—I knew.*
> Life has made clear to me
>   That, strive but for closer view,
> *Love were as plain to see.*
>
> " When see ? When there dawns a day,
>   If not on the homely earth,
> Then yonder, worlds away,
>   Where the strange and new have birth,
> And Power comes full in play."

Could the poet have given us a nobler dying song than this ? It is one of his noblest yet tenderest utterances—the refrain of which is : " God is Love."

It has been remarked the outcome of the poem of *Easter Day* is found in one of its concluding lines : "I find it hard to be a Christian." But the poet assuredly does not mean by that statement that he finds it hard to grasp the facts of our Saviour's Divine and personal relation to all mankind, but *hard to live the divinely Christian life,*—the utter selflessness and self-abnegation that following Christ involves ; hard to live that broad, tolerant, sympathetic, large-hearted, unique life of love that being a Christian implies : for the poet concludes with a magnificent outburst of triumphant music, in which his soul seems to glow like the flush of a sunset sky, and his spirit rises grand with the grandeur of a full-orbed faith :

> " But Easter-Day breaks ! But
> Christ rises ! Mercy every way
> Is infinite,—and who can say ? "

He is sure of the Resurrection—then he is sure of Christ, "And who can say ?" Say what ? Why, what the possibilities of the race will yet be, in that higher, greater, and holier sphere, where the living Christ shall be a living and loving Guide to all human hearts for ever.

But with the *Death in the Desert* before us, one cannot long remain in doubt as to the directness of Mr. Browning's distinctively Christian teaching ; and which is brought out

still more decisively perhaps in *Saul.* Here
Mr. Browning is supreme and at his best ; and
his utterance comes very close to the prophetic :

> " Oh, speak through me now !
> Would I suffer for him that I love ? So would'st thou,
>   —so wilt thou ! . . . . .
> He who did most, shall bear most ; the strongest shall
>   stand the most weak.
> 'Tis the weakness in strength, that I cry for ! my flesh,
>   that I seek   [be
> In the Godhead ! I seek and I find it—O Saul, it shall
> A Face like my face that receives thee ; a Man like to
>   me,
> Thou shalt love and be loved by, for ever: a Hand like
>   this hand
> Shall throw open the gates of new life to thee ! *See the
>   Christ stand !* "

Since Mr. Browning's death there has been
published in the *Nonconformist* a singularly
beautiful letter written by him in 1876, which,
emphasizes our poet's attitudes towards Christianity.   Mr. Browning, received a letter from
a lady who, believing herself to be dying,
wrote to thank him for the help she had derived
from his poems, mentioning particularly *Rabbi
Ben Ezra* and *Abt Vogler,* and expressing the
deep satisfaction she felt that one so highly
endowed with genius held to the cardinal
truths of religion, and he replied as follows :

> " 19, Warwick Crescent, W.,
> Dear Friend,   *May* 11, '76.
>   It would ill become me to waste a

word on my own feelings except inasmuch
as they can be common to us both, in such a
situation as you describe yours to be, and
which, by sympathy, I can make mine by the
anticipation of a few years at most. It is a
great thing, the greatest, that a human being
should have passed the probation of life, and
sum up its experience in a witness to the
power and love of God. I dare congratulate
you. All the help I can offer, in my poor degree, is the assurance that I see ever *more*
reason to hold by the same hope—and that
by no means in ignorance of what has been
advanced to the contrary ; and for your sake
I would wish it to be true that I had so much
of 'genius' as to permit the testimony of an
especially privileged insight to come in aid
of the ordinary argument. For I know I, myself, have been aware of the communication of
something more subtle than a ratiocinative
process, when the convictions of 'genius' have
thrilled my soul to its depths, as when Napo-
leon, shutting up the New Testament, said of
Christ : "Do you know that I am an under-
stander of men ? Well, He was no man ! "
('Savez-vous que je me connais en hommes ?
Eh bien, celui-là ne fut pas un homme.') Or
as when Charles Lamb, in a gay fancy with
some friends as to how he and they would feel
if the greatest of the dead were to appear suddenly in flesh and blood once more, on the
final suggestion, " And if Christ entered this

room ?" changed his manner at once, and
stuttered out, as his manner was when moved,
"You see, if Shakespeare entered we should
all rise; if *He* appeared we must kneel." Or,
not to multiply instances, as when Dante wrote
what I will transcribe from my wife's Testament, wherein I recorded it fourteen years ago,
"Thus I believe, thus I affirm, thus I am certain it is, that from this life I shall pass to
another better, there, where that lady lives of
whom my soul was enamoured."* Dear friend,
I may have wearied you in spite of your good
will. God bless you, sustain, and receive you !
Reciprocate this blessing with

Yours affectionately,
ROBERT BROWNING."

This brings us to *Prospice*, magnificent in
its triumph-note, fearless in faith, undaunted
in courage. Hope, Love, Faith,—these have
stood him in good stead through the days of

---

* Two years after the date of this letter, appeared
Mr. Browning's *La Saisiaz*, in which the following lines
occur :—

> "I take upon my lips
> Phrase the solemn Tuscan fashioned, and declare the
>   soul's eclipse
> Not the soul's extinction. Take his—'I believe and I
>   declare—
> Certain am I—from this life I pass into a better, there
> Where this lady lives of whom enamoured was my
>   soul.'"

his life.   His friends have left him; the one
Love of his soul has passed from his sight, and
left him solitary and alone, pacing the shores
of Time : still, he has not left go of Hope,
and Trust yet walks by his side through the
busy world of men.   But at last comes Death
—how now?   Can he still "hope on, hold
hard in the subtle thing that's spirit"?   Is
there any fear touching his heart?   Listen to
his triumphant response :

" Fear death ?—to feel the fog in my throat,
    The mist in my face,
When the snows begin, and the blasts denote
    I am nearing the place,
The power of the night, the press of the storm,
    The post of the foe ;
Where he stands, the Arch Fear in a visible form,
    Yet the strong man must go :
For the journey is done and the summit attained,
    And the barriers fall,
Though a battle's to fight ere the guerdon be gained,
    The reward of it all.
I was ever a fighter, so—one fight more,
    The best and the last !   [bore,
I would hate that death bandaged my eyes, and for-
    And bade me creep past.
No ! let me taste the whole of it, fare like my peers
    The heroes of old,
Bear the brunt, in a minute pay glad life's arrears
    Of pain, darkness and cold.
For sudden the worst turns the best to the brave,
    The black minute's at end,
And the elements' rage, the fiend-voices that rave,
    Shall dwindle, shall blend,
Shall change, shall become first a peace out of pain,
    Then a light, then thy breast,

O thou soul of my soul ! I shall clasp thee again,
  And with God be the rest ! "

Browning, as will appear from the above letter, was not afraid to grapple with " doubt " —indeed, he *has* grappled with it, and has come out victorious : he knows that *earnest* doubt is but a stepping stone to the highest faith. As *Bishop Blougram* has it :

" You call for faith :
I show you doubt, to prove that faith exists,
The more of doubt, the stronger faith, I say,
If faith o'ercomes doubt. How I know it does ?
By life and man's free will, God gave for that ! . . .

The reader, in this connection, may refer to that lovely little poem, *Fears and Scruples*, but more especially to *Abt Vogler.* In reading this poem, one's step gathers strength with the strength of the verse ; one's heart expands with the glow of faith and the perfect serenity of the poet's vision ; and one is able to realise to the full the blessedness and joy of belief, and to exclaim, " Thank God, I am a man, with all a man's imperfection, and tendency to doubt, yet able to say with the poet —'let doubt occasion still more faith.' " It is this manly, strong teaching that our age needs ; and it is this that alone will save it from the pessimistic influences that seem ever to encircle one's path. The musician, *Abt Vogler,* while extemporising on a musical instrument of his own invention, has built up a mighty

palace of sound, wonderful, weird, beautiful ;
he wishes his music could become a *visible*
palace of beauty, but, lo, it all vanishes, and
he ends his "extemporising" by seeing in
the incompleteness of sound—its effect ceas-
ing with silence, an earnest of completeness
by and bye, completeness in that infinite blue,
where no failure will ever be writ, no "lost
hope" ever recorded :

Therefore to whom turn I but to Thee, the ineffable
    Name?
  Builder and Maker, Thou, of houses not made with
    hands.
What, have fear of change from Thee who art ever the
    same?
  Doubt that Thy power can fill the heart that Thy
    power expands?
There shall never be one lost good! What was, shall
    live as before;
  The evil is null, is nought, is silence implying sound;
What was good, shall be good, with, for evil, so much
    good more—
  On the earth the broken arcs ; in the heaven, a per-
    fect round.

VI.

To pass now to another phase of Mr. Browning's art: in the poet's conception of life, Love occupies a prominent place. No life is perfect without love—but it must be a love that will regenerate; not the false sentiment so often mistaken for love: the *true* love is the love that influences for good another life; not the love that kindles passion, but the love that inspires nobleness, devoutness, faith—in a word, *soul-love*. Without this, human life is incomplete; with it, there is an ever-present joy and blessedness. The mere love for the sake of gaining love's reward—the winning of the loved one's hand—is but a small matter. The true love is the love for *love's sake*, without thought of possible reward: for, says Mr. Browning, there can be but *one love in a life*—it is once and for ever and never again. Marriage may or may not follow, but love is love, and is eternal. Here are some beautiful lines from a fascinating play, *Colombe's Birthday*, written by Browning nine and thirty years since. Valence, a poor advocate of Cleves, has fallen in love with the Duchess, to whom he has gone to present a petition, and who, of course, is socially far above him, and unapproachable by him. This love having been eventually discovered, it appears that the Duchess has likewise learned to love him; thereupon his fellows are ready enough to taunt him that, so far as *he* is concerned, *love* can have little place in the matter; it is her *hand*, not her *heart*, he aspires to. But he proudly answers them :

" Who thought upon reward ? And yet how much
Comes after—oh, what amplest recompense !
Is the *knowledge* of her naught ? The *memory* naught ?
—Lady, should such an one have looked on you,
Ne'er wrong yourself so far as quote the world
And say. love can go unrequited here !
You will have blessed him to his whole life's end—
Low passions hindered, baser cares kept back,
All goodness cherished, where you dwelt and dwell."

And the same idea occurs in an earlier play, *Strafford*, where Lady Carlisle exclaims :

" Ah, have I spared
Strafford a pang, and *shall I seek reward*
Beyond that memory ? Surely, too, *some way*
He is the better for my love."

See, too, how noble is Browning's view of love in the little poem, *One way of Love*. The orthodox poet, with unrequited love, would have sobbed out his sorrows in the world's ear ; would cultivate sentimentalities as he bemoaned his forlorn condition : not so the true poet, as typified by Browning; the thing that would engender that feeling is not

love, but passion : here is the higher ideal of
love under like circumstances—

" All June I bound the rose in sheaves,
   Now, rose by rose, I strip the leaves,
   And strew them where Pauline may pass.
   She will not turn aside ? Alas !
   Let them lie. Suppose they die ?
   The chance was they might take her eyé.

How many a mouth I strove to suit
   These stubborn fingers to the lute !
   To-day I venture all I know.
   She will not hear my music ? So !
   Break the string ; fold music's wing ;
   Suppose Pauline had bade me sing !

My whole life long I learned to love.
   This hour my utmost art I prove
   And speak my passion—heaven or hell ?
   She will not give me heaven ? 'Tis well !
   Lose who may—I still can say,
   Those who win heaven, blest are they ! "

He is the better man for that love of his, although another has stepped in before him and
obtained the prize. Those who *have* gained
life's prize of love, blest are they ; still, he too,
who has failed, has gained somewhat, *for he
has loved*, and all his life through he will be the
nobler and happier man for that one revelation : he will have gained a greater than
happiness, even (as Carlyle has it) *blessedness :*
a truly noble way this, of "falling in love."

   Then, says Browning, finding love *here*, the
lover will soon get to look through and be-

yond it to love *there :* that is, that through
the earthly love he will seek the heavenly ;
so that, should he apparently fail here in
love's quest, his life has been neither aimless
nor hopeless, for his so-called failure will lead
him to the highest love—that is, God's. The
reader may, in this connection, turn to two
little poems in the first series of selections :
Love in a Life and *Life in a Love.* I am
aware that it is rather hazardous to send the
"beginner" to these poems, as they are generally looked upon as peculiarly obscure ; but
a little patience will show that what the poet
has to teach here is, that the highest love cannot be included in a *life ;* but that, on the
other hand, the best and noblest life *is* sus-
tained by a great love ; and is carried onward
and upward to "other heights in other lives."

> "But what if I fail in my purpose here ?
>   It is but to keep the nerves at strain,
>   To dry one's eyes and laugh at a fall,
>   And baffled, get up and begin again—
>   So the chase takes up one's life, that's all."

So with *Pompilia* and *Caponsacchi.* To the
outside world their life is a failure. They met
—loved—

> "Understood each other at first look"—

but the world's barriers are between them, and
duty speaks. Is their love a failure then ?

was it better they should never have met—
or met, gone their various ways regardless one
of the other ? Assuredly not ; for they *have*
loved ; and life is perfected by love ! Shall
we think of them, then, as having *failed*—as
having lost the compensations of life—been
cheated, as it were, by Time ? Nay: their
love in Time but grows, ripens, and develops
—till its fruition in Eternity. Love is not
lost ; but is an ever-present help to the soul
left to carry on the struggle alone. Let me
close this section with *Pompilia's* noble words :

My end of breath
Shall bear away my soul in being true !
He is still here, not outside with the world,
Here, here, I have him in his rightful place !
'Tis now, when I am most upon the move,
I feel for what I verily find—again
The face, again the eyes, again, through all,
The heart and its immeasurable love
Of my one friend, my only, all my own,
Who put his breast between the spears and me.
Ever with Caponsacchi ! Otherwise
Here alone would be failure, loss to me—
How much more loss to him, with life debarred
From giving life, love locked from love's display,
The day-star stopped its task that makes night morn!
O lover of my life, O soldier saint
No work begun shall ever pause for death !
Love will be helpful to me more and more
I' the coming course, the new path I must tread,
My weak hand in thy strong hand, strong for that.

VII.

As many of my readers probably know little
of Mr. Browning's poetry, we will analyse one
or two of the leading shorter poems, and endeavour to prove to them that, with a little
patience, Mr. Browning is easily understand-
able.

I would advise beginners to obtain the
first volume of *Selections*,* in which they
will find some of the poet's best and most
characteristic work ; and for the further
reason that, in the study of these poems, it is
absolutely essential that the student should
" begin in the right class." No doubt much
of the feeling as to Browning's obscurity
arises from the fact that the reader began
where he should have ended. He took up
perhaps some of his later works, in which there
are (as the greatest lovers of Browning will
admit) many difficulties, and was naturally
repelled and discouraged from further at-

---

* *Selections from the Poetry of Robert Browning.*
Two vols. Smith, Elder and Co. The "beginner" will
find these volumes (he should, I think, begin with the
first) a fitting prelude to the study of Browning's completed work ; and all readers of modern English poetry
are certainly indebted to the publishers for this cheap
and capital selection.

tempts ; but if he will begin with the earlier and shorter poems, he will gradually grow accustomed to the poet's style, will be prepared to exert that intelligence which Browning certainly does demand of the reader, and will soon learn to love his strong and vigorous lines, to make them part of his own mental nature, and having *learned to love*, and grown into the meaning and mystery of Browning's strong sentences, he will find that no English writer is at once so vigorous, so bold, so healthy ; that the poet stands alone and unrivalled, as a great, strong, robust soul—whose verse eats into our very heart and mind.

One of the first poems which will probably attract the beginner, is the *Lost Leader.* The fire and *verve* of this fine lyric will at once make itself apparent ; and while many readers will fit the lines to some " lost leader " of their own, the question will naturally occur, " who was in the poet's mind when he wrote the poem ?" Most readers of Browning are no doubt aware, that for a long time the question was debated as to whether Wordsworth was not the " lost leader ; " but the question has been finally set at rest by the poet himself, who, in 1875, wrote to Dr. Grosart as follows :

" I have been asked the question you now address me with, and as duly answered it, I can't remember how many times: there is no sort of objection to one more assurance, or

rather confession, on my part, that I *did* in
my hasty youth presume to use the great and
venerated personality of Wordsworth as a sort
of painter's model, one from which this or the
other particular feature may be selected, and
turned to account : had I intended more, above
all, such a boldness as portraying the entire
man, I should not have talked about ' handfuls
of silver and bits of riband.'   These never influenced the change of politics in the great
poet ; whose defection, nevertheless, accompanied as it was by a regular face-about of his
special party, was to my juvenile apprehension, and even mature consideration, an event
to deplore.   But just as in the tapestry on my
wall I can recognize figures which have *struck
out* a fancy, on occasion, that though truly
enough thus derived, yet would be preposter-
ous as a copy, so, though I dare not deny the
original of my little poem, I altogether refuse
to have it considered as the ' very effigies ' of
such a moral and intellectual superiority."

Of whom was Wordsworth the "lost leader"?
Presumably of the little band who, at the beginning of the present century, led the struggle
that had for its supreme object liberty of
thought, and the universal brotherhood of the
race ; the band which appeared to have lost
its one possible leader when Shelley perished
in that fatal storm in the gulf of Spezzia :

Wordsworth being the one Englishman who
could have carried on the work.

" We that had loved him so, followed him, honoured
    him,
  Lived in his mild and magnificent eye,
Learned his great language, caught his clear accents,
  Made him our pattern to live and to die.
Shakespeare was of us, Milton was for us,
  Burns, Shelley, were with us—they watch from their
    graves !
He alone breaks from the van and the freemen,
  He alone sinks to the rear and the slaves ! "

It is noteworthy that the poet, in his mature
age, should still deplore the abandonment by
Wordsworth of the cause which makes for
freedom and liberty.

The student may now turn to another lyric,
perhaps the finest of its kind in the language,
The Last Ride Together, and he will not fail
to note the measured pulsing of the lines,
which seem to keep time to the horses' gallop.
The lover has loved in vain ; youth has passed
in the quest ; and he now resigns himself to
his fate—but ere he does this he begs for one
last ride with his beloved ; and during the ride
he reflects on success or failure in life. He
has failed ; but what then ?

" Fail I alone, in words and deeds ?
  Why, all men strive and who succeeds ?
  We rode ; it seemed my spirits flew,
  Saw other regions, cities new,
    As the world rushed by on either side.

I thought,—All labour, yet no less
Bear up beneath their unsuccess.
Look at the end of work, contrast
The petty done, the undone vast,
This present of their's with the hopeful past !
 I hoped she would love me ; here we ride."

Then there flashes through his mind the
idea that were success achieved here, if
one obtained the full fruition of one's hopes
and desires in this life of limitation, what need
would there be for heaven ; nay, would one
care for heaven at all ?   This thought brings
a feeling of rest to his spirit, and as he dreams
of riding with his love for " ever and ever," he
questions with himself whether *this* may not
be heaven :

" And yet—she has not spoke so long !
 What if heaven be that, fair and strong
 At life's best, with our eyes upturned,
 Whither life's flower is first discerned,
  We, fixed so, ever should so abide !
 What if we still ride on, we two,
 With life for ever old yet new,
 Changed not in kind but in degree,
 The instant made eternity,—
 And heaven just prove that I and she
  Ride, ride together, forever ride !"

We will next take up a lyrical gem of the
first water, *A Woman's last word,* which
explains itself.   There has evidently been a
" misunderstanding " between husband and
wife ; and the " woman " is having the " last

word "—a word of infinite tenderness and self
surrender.

> " Let's contend no more, Love,
>   Strive nor weep :
> All be as before, Love,
>   Only sleep !   .   .   . .
>
> Teach me, only teach, Love !
>   As I ought
> I will speak thy speech, Love,
>   Think thy thought—
>
> Meet, if thou require it,
>   Both demands,
> Laying flesh and spirit
>   In thy hands !
>
> That shall be to-morrow,
>   Not to-night :
> I must bury sorrow
>   Out of sight :
>
> Must a little weep, Love
>   (Foolish me !)
> And so fall asleep, Love,
>   Loved by thee."

Somewhat in the same strain, we next hear
a man's voice—a strong, healthy note, though
full of a yearning tenderness—in a longer poem,
called *A Lover's Quarrel.* This is easily under-
standable, and contains some exquisite poetry.

> " Dearest, three months ago
> When we loved each other so,
>   Lived and loved the same,
>   Till an evening came,
> When a shaft from the devil's bow
>   Pierced to our ingle-glow,
> And the friends were friend and foe !

Woman, and will you cast
For a word, quite off at last
 Me, your own, your You,
 Since, as truth is true,
I was You all the happy Past—
 Me do you leave aghast
With the memories We amassed?

Love, if you knew the light
That your soul casts in my sight,
 How I look to you
 For the pure and true,
And the beauteous and the right—
 Bear with a moment's spite
When a mere mote threats the white ! "

There is a quiet, brooding thoughtfulness in that retrospective-like poem entitled *By the Fireside.* It is a very beautiful creation, full of pure, manly feeling and emotion, and is dear to all lovers of our poet ; the verses read as though written in the very presence of that peerless singer, Elizabeth Barrett Browning :

" My perfect wife, my Leonor,
 Oh heart, my own, oh eyes, mine too,
Whom else could I dare look forward for,
 With whom beside should I dare pursue
The path grey heads abhor ?

My own, confirm me ! If I tread
 This path back, is it not in pride
To think how little I dreamed it led
 To an age so blest that, by its side
Youth seems the waste indeed ?

Think, when our one soul understands
　　The great Word which makes all things new,
When earth breaks up and heaven expands,
　　How will the change strike me and you
In the house not made with hands?

Oh I must feel your brain prompt mine,
　　Your heart anticipate my heart,
You must be just before, in fine,
　　See and make me see, for your part,
New depths of the divine!"

There is a longer poem in this first volume of *Selections*, which the beginner may now take up, and which is charged to the full with fire and poetry—I refer to the *Flight of the Duchess*. This strong poem gives a rare insight into Browning's sharp, incisive lines, into his marvellous power in the manipulation of rhyme, and his fervid imagination. It is full of a strange and subtle music—weird and ghost-like as a setting of Wagner's: the opening stanzas display all Browning's unique power of *realism*—one can *see* the scene he is describing. It is indeed a "great wild country,"—leading out past the cornfields and vineyards, to cattle track and open chase, till the base of the mountain is reached, where

　　　"At a funeral pace
Round about, solemn and slow,
One by one, row after row,
Up and up the pine trees go,　 . . .
And so on, more and ever more,
Till at the last for a bounding belt,
Comes the salt sand hoar of the great sea shore."

The poem is, as I have said, full of music, and the words of the Gipsy Queen in this poem glow with a strangely fascinating melody; the whole culminating in one note of high-wrought pathos, when, on the topmost height of "old age," the poet, glancing back on the Past, is about to open the veil into the Unseen and Eternal:

So, at the last shall come old age,
Decrepit as befits that stage;
How else wouldst thou retire apart.
With the hoarded memories of thy heart,
And gather all to the very least
Of the fragments of life's earlier feast,
Let fall through eagerness to find
The crowning dainties yet behind?
Ponder on the entire past
Laid together thus at last,
When the twilight helps to fuse
The first fresh with the faded hues,
And the outline of the whole,
As round eve's shades their framework roll,
Grandly fronts for once thy soul.
And then, as 'mid the dark, a gleam
Of yet another morning breaks,
And, like the hand which ends a dream,
Death, with the might of his sunbeam,
Touches the flesh, and the soul awakes,
Then ———."

"Then" ——— Alas, the poet can take us no further; he has brought to the very vestibule of the House of God; we long to hear what more he has to reveal to us of the glories

within ; our ears are strained to their utmost
tension, but, ah, the inevitable "but" appals
us once again; and we, like the poet, with
brave hearts and chastened spirits, must do
our appointed tasks on this earth—awaiting
His time ere we, too, ascend "those other
heights in other lives."

But for pathos, for emotion, for all those
holy feelings that come right home to the human heart, the poem entitled *Any Wife to any
Husband* is incomparable and unique. Let
the student read it through quietly and
thoughtfully, once, twice, three times, and he
will assuredly rise with a feeling of awe and
reverence, intensified by each successive reading, and will claim for the poet not merely the
title of singer, but of teacher, consoler, and
friend. A true wife, whose whole life has
been wrapped up in the love of her husband,
is dying ; she knows that she is fading, that her
life is slowly ebbing away—that she must
leave him who was and is all and in all to her ;
and in these last supreme moments she utters
forth her heart to him—who, too, has loved
her right well, and who is sobbing out his soul
by her dying bed. She tells him how sure
she is of his love ; she never had a doubt
about *that*—

> "I have but to be by thee, and thy hand
> Will never let mine go, nor heart withstand
> The beating of my heart to reach its place.

> When shall I look for thee and feel thee gone?
> When cry for the old comfort and find none?
> Never, I know! Thy soul is in thy face."

She feels that her human beauty is fading—
her face is getting thinner, the lines of care
and suffering are writing themselves on her
noble brow; and with all a woman's true
instinct she would have saved *that* for *his sake* :

> "Oh, I should fade—'tis willed so! Might I save,
> Gladly I would, whatever beauty gave
> Joy to thy sense, for that was precious too.
> It is not to be granted. But the soul
> Whence the love comes, all ravage leaves that whole ;
> Vainly the flesh fades ; soul makes all things new."

Ah, but when she is gone, will he still love her,
on and on into the new life whither she has fled?
Will he remain faithful to her memory? No ;
she knows he will not. All those dear words
and tendernesses once uttered to her will be
passed on to another:

> "Ah! but the fresher faces! 'Is it true,'
> Thou'lt ask, 'some eyes are beautiful and new?
> Some hair—how can one choose but grasp such
>   wealth?
> And if a man would press his lips to lips,
> Fresh as the wilding hedge-rose-cup there slips
> The dew-drop out of, must it be by stealth?
> 'It cannot change the love still kept *for Her.*'

> "So must I see, from where I sit and watch,
> My own self sell myself, my hand attach
> Its warrant to the very thefts from me—
> Thy singleness of soul that made me proud,
> Thy purity of heart I loved aloud,
> Thy man's truth I was bold to bid God see !"

Still, for her as for all, *true* love is eternal and unchangeable; that is only the outer shell that can be given to another: the real essence of man's own being—all that love means and is—can be but given to *one*, and must and shall be hers for ever. And thus will he come back to her again in the land of Light and Love, when earth's shadows shall be dissolved in the sunlight of eternal beauty.

" It all comes to the same thing at the end,
    Since mine thou wast, mine art, and mine shalt be;
 Faithful or faithless : sealing up the sum
 Or lavish of my treasure, thou must come
    Back to the heart's place here I keep for thee !

" Only why should it be with stain at all ?
 Why must I, 'twixt the leaves of coronal,
    Put any kiss of pardon on thy brow ?
 Why need the other women know so much,
 And talk together, Such the look and such
    The smile he used to love with, then as now !

" Might I die last and show thee ! Should I find
 Such hardship in the few years left behind,
    If free to take and light my lamp and go
 Into thy tomb, and shut the door and sit,
 Seeing thy face on those four sides of it
    The better that they are so blank, I know ! "

But, in spite of all, she sees, with the intuitive and unerring vision of the dying, that he will, after all that she can say, be faithless to her memory—choosing one of the " fresher faces;" and so the poem closes with a last appeal on her part—surely one of the most pathetic, simple, yet withal beautiful poems in our English literature.

Andrea del Sarto is a poem dear and precious to all readers of Browning. It is an "imaginary conversation," an altogether beautiful picture : while some of the poet's highest teaching is to be found in it. The great painter is pleading with his wife—pleading that she would return to him some of the love that *he* lavishes upon her; that she would give to him the *incentive* to work for the sake of art and the glory—not for the mere worldly gain. Oh, how different would his life then be ! With his hand in hers, tenderly does he plead with her :

> "I often am much wearier than you think,
> This evening, more than usual : and it seems
> As if—forgive me—should you let me sit;
> Here by the window, with your hand in mine,
> And look a half-hour forth on Fiesole,
> Both of one mind, as married people use,
> Quietly, quietly, the evening through,
> I might get up to-morrow to my work,
> Cheerful and fresh as ever. Let us try.

Then he proceeds to speak of the failure of his work. He is called the "*Faultless*" painter—but on that very ground his work fails ; perfection cannot be attained in this life of limitation : no man can say he has *here*, in this life, attained to his ideal—for there is still an ideal beyond the ideal. Mark well these pregnant lines :

> "Ah, but a man's reach should exceed his grasp,
> Or what's a heaven for? All is silver grey,
> Placid and perfect with my art : the worse !"

We are not to be content with what we can grasp, but reach after something *beyond* our grasp ; or, in other words, we are not to be content with this limited life and its cares ; but to strive after the eternal life—the only *real* life. So he goes on pleading with the woman whom he loves (and who is even then thinking of another than he) :

" But had you—oh, with the same perfect brow,
  And perfect eyes, and more than perfect mouth,
  And the low voice my soul hears, as a bird
  The fowler's pipe, and follows to the snare—
  Had you with these the same, but brought a mind !
  Some women do so.   Had the mouth there urged
  ' God and the glory ! never care for gain.
  The present by the future, what is that ?
  Live for fame, side by side with Agnolo !
  Rafael is waiting : up to God all three !'
  I might have done it for you."

Another vivid piece of portraiture in this first series of selections is *An Epistle*, narrating the " strange medical experience of Karshish, the Arab physician."   Karshish, the " picker-up of learning's crumbs," in the course of his travels comes to Bethany, from whence he writes to his teacher Abib, giving an account of his many wanderings.   Among the numberless strange things that have befallen him, is none other than a meeting with " one Lazarus, a Jew, sanguine, proportioned, fifty years of age," whose strange medical " case " was a sort of mania,—" a trance prolonged unduly some three days,"

" And first—the man's own firm conviction rests
That he was dead (in fact, they buried him)—
That he was dead, and then restored to life
By a Nazarene physician of his tribe :
—Sayeth, the same bade ' Rise,' and he did rise !"

Then follows a vivid description of how Lazarus views the world after his three days' sleep :

" Whence has the man the balm that brightens all ?
This grown man eyes the world now like a child.
Some elders of his tribe, I should premise,
Led in their friend, obedient as a sheep,
To bear my inquisition.   While they spoke,
Now sharply, now with sorrow,—told the case—
He listened not except I spoke to him,
But folded his two hands, and let them talk,
Watching the flies that buzzed : and yet no fool.
And that's a sample how his years must go."

Now we have a picture of the life led by the
risen Lazarus—of the wonderful sense of God
in the man's soul :

"And oft the man's soul springs into his face
As if he saw again and heard again,
His sage that bade him ' Rise ' and he did rise.
Indeed, the especial marking of the man
Is prone submission to the heavenly will,
Seeing it, what it is, and why it is—
'Sayeth, he will wait patient to the last—
He will live, nay, it pleaseth him to live
So long as God please, and just how God please."

The thought then occurs to Karshish, that his
teacher Abib will inquire why he did not seek
out the sage—but he anticipates the question,

and says, " Alas, he perished in a tumult long ago." At this point, the physician bursts out into a sudden indignation at what he has heard, and comes to the conclusion that this Lazarus must be just stark mad :

" This man so cured regards the Curer, then
　As—God forgive me ! who but God himself,
　Creator and sustainer of the world,
　That came and dwelt in flesh on it awhile—
　Taught, healed the sick, broke bread at his own
　　house,
　Then died, with Lazarus by, for aught I know,
　And yet was . . . . what I said nor choose repeat."

Astonished at his own credulity in listening to this Jew's tale, Karshish begs pardon of the learned leech, his master, for dwelling on it at such length ; but suddenly, at the close of his letter, the whole truth seems to dawn on him. There *must* be something in it ; the story cannot be all a lie—and he exclaims :

" The very God ! think Abib ; dost thou think ?
　So, the All-Great, were the All-Loving, too—
　So, through the thunder comes a human voice
　Saying, ' O heart I made, a heart beats here !
　' Face, my hands fashioned, see it in myself !
　' Thou hast no power nor mayest conceive of mine ;
　' But love I gave thee, with myself to love,
　' And thou must love me who have died for thee ! '
　The madman saith He said so : it is strange ! "

Here is another poem,—the *Boy and the Angel*, commencing :

　　" Morning, evening, noon, and night,
　　" Praise God," sang Theocrite.

I

Theocrite was but a poor little fellow, who, in his narrow cell, had to work hard during the long hours of the day, earning his bread. But the boy was happy, for he was always singing God's praise :

> " Hard he laboured, long and well,
>   O'er his work the boy's curls fell.
>   But ever at each period
>   He stopped, and sang ' Praise God ! '
>   Then back again his curls he threw,
>   And cheerful turned to work anew."

But Theocrite, like all boys, thought he could do better things were he only a great man ; and so he wished to become the Pope, that he might be enabled to praise God better, and God granted him his wish. The boy falls ill, and appears to die, and when he awakens he finds himself Pope. But the boy's cell is empty, and God "misses his little human praise ; " and so the angel Gabriel is sent to take the boy's place. But no ; the song of the great angel is not so sweet to God as was that of the little boy. The angelic song is beautiful, but far more beautiful and dear to God is the human praise. When that little voice stayed its singing, it seemed as though the chorus of creation had stopped too. So the new Pope, Theocrite, becomes the boy again, Gabriel becoming Pope instead.

The beginner may now take up *Saul*,—incomparably the finest lyric in modern poetry—brimful of music. David has been sent to Saul that he might sing and play to him, and deliver him from the terrible inward conflict that is consuming him ; and as he sings, he unburthens himself, utters strange prophecies, and tells of a Christ to come. More severe in style, but in its way as beautiful, is *The Death in the Desert*—a poem of wondrous power. The beloved Apostle is dying in the desert, hidden in the inmost recesses of a cave —his companions, four disciples and a boy. Outside, where one kept watch, " was all noon, and the burning blue ; " but within the cool of the cave, the dying John utters his last words —words of infinite pathos and beauty, full of impressive power. Growing more and more prophetic, the dying apostle rises into " farsounding melody of strength," as in his rapt vision he sees the far-off time, when men will be eagerly inquiring, " Did John live at all ? and did he say he *saw* the Christ ? "   It is a poem the age needs, and one that should be pondered over by the thoughtful student. Then there is the *Confessional ; Evelyn Hope* —a poem to be treasured in one's heart as a sacred memory ; *Love among the Ruins ; Two in the Campagna; Home Thoughts from Abroad; The Statue and the Bust ; The Guardian Angel ; Cleon ; James Lee's Wife ; In a Gondola ; Caliban upon Setebos*, a sermon upon the text, " Thou thoughtest that I was altogether such an one as thyself " ; *The Italian in England*—a poem which Mazzini once read

to his fellow-exiles to show how an Englishman could sympathize with them—and many
others; with all of which the beginner may
readily become familiar and will easily understand.

And now the student will, I think, be
ready to acknowledge the wealth and power
to be found in the works of Robert Browning,
and I can leave him to wander at will in
this newly-discovered country.   He can, if he
prefer, leave *Sordello* till the last, but he is by
no means to be deterred from giving it at
least two or three readings; but he can now
take up *Paracelsus, Christmas Eve and Easter
Day, La Saisiaz,* the two series of *Dramatic
Idylls* and *Jocoseria, Ferishtah's Fancies,* and
the plays—especially *Colombe's Birthday, The
Blot in the 'Scutcheon* (containing, as Arch-
deacon Farrar has said, the sweetest love poem
in the English language); *Strafford* and *In a
Balcony,* with the many other works of our
beloved master.

In many of these poems, the reader will find
Mr. Browning's sense of humour strongly
brought out—and it is a humour of a rare and
unique kind.   He will note it especially in *A
Soul's Tragedy,* and in *Fra Lippo;* but it is
indeed scattered more or less over much of his
work, and may be spoken of as one of his chief
characteristics as a poet.

Since Emerson and Carlyle wrote, no man
has come to us charged with a more earnest

message to his fellows that Robert Browning.
To him work is not the all and in all of life—
there is work of the soul as of the body ; and
his anathemas are hurled with no unsparing
hand against mere worldliness, and the
"getting-on-in-life" doctrines. Here is his
rebuke to those who *live*, in a double sense, in
their shops, and exist only to accumulate gain,
having no finer aspirations of the spirit to
keep alive their inner and higher life :

> " Because a man has shop to mind
>   In time and place, since flesh must live,
> Needs spirit lack all life behind,
>   All stray thoughts, fancies fugitive,
>   All loves except what trade can give ?
>
> I want to know a butcher paints,
>   A baker rhymes for his pursuit,
> Candlestick-maker much acquaints
>   His soul with song, or, haply mute,
>   Blows out his brains upon the flute.
>
> But—shop each day and all day long !
>   Friend, your good angel slept, your star
> Suffered eclipse, fate did you wrong !
>   From where these sorts of treasures are,
>   There should our hearts be—Christ, how far

VII.

HAVING got so far into the study of Mr. Browning's work, the reader may now turn to the Poet's masterpiece—*The Ring and the Book*. He will doubtless have been eager to have dipped into this colossal poem at a less advanced stage of his studies, the more especially as he may have heard it spoken of as containing a story of absorbing interest, and as being less obscure than many of the other poems. But it is, I think, essential that the student should know something of Mr. Browning's earlier work ere he takes up his *chef d'œuvre ;* for from *Paracelsus* onward to *Men and Women* and *Dramatis Personæ* there is a gradual development, both in poetic art and evolution of thought, which culminates in *The Ring and the Book*. This is the high-water mark of Mr. Browning's literary career—the work which crowned him "chief poet of the age"; all the characters of his genius are here displayed—passion, pathos and humour, strength and beauty, a marvellous analytical and psychological power, combined with a prodigality of thought, and a dramatic force and *verve*, truly astonishing. It is undoubtedly, looked at from all sides, the greatest poem of the century; nay, the greatest since the dramas of Shakespeare. It stands alone in its uniqueness ; there is nothing like it in English literature—for it is *human* to the core ; it is indeed a precious possession to the soul of man, revealing, as it does, the ultimate triumph of right over wrong, of good over evil, of truth over falsehood.

The poet tells us how, one day, strolling across a Square in Florence, he stopped at a book-stall, and suddenly pounced upon an old volume, "part print, part manuscript," which contained an account of the trial of one Count Guido Franceschini and his four accomplices for the murder of his wife Pompilia, and her putative parents, Pietro and Violante Comparini. At once he bought it—gave a *lira* for it —"eightpence English just," and discovered in his purchase the story of a tragedy of intense human interest.

To give the reader some "general idea" of the plot of this poem, I will put lightly together the leading features of the story, as found by the poet in this old book. With these in his mind, the consecutive narratives, as told by the various *dramatis personæ* will be more easily followed.

Some two hundred years ago, there lived in the Via Vittoria, Rome, two people of "the modest middle class," Pietro and Violante Comparini. Pietro was possessed of "house and land," and also had "moneys' use lifelong," —which, in the event of his dying without heirs

passed out of his family. Therefore his one
grief was the old grief—he had no child. After
some years, however, his wife Violante—

> "'Twixt a smile and a blush
> With touch of agitation proper too,
> Announced that, spite of her unpromising age
> The miracle would in time be manifest,
> An heir's birth was to happen : and it did."

And in time the event came to pass : a baby
girl was shown to old Pietro, the simple
fellow being beside himself with joy. The
child—named Pompilia—was tenderly brought
up by the good old man, who loved her as his
life ; and who, rapt up in the joy of possessing
this new treasure, spent most of his time in
play ; until, at the end of twelve years—he
having in the meantime "learned to dandle
and forgot to dig"—poverty "reached him in
her rounds." In this strait, Violante, as one
said, spied out "Count Guido Franceschini,
the Aretine," threw "her bait, Pompilia,"
and caught the noble. So, one day, in her
thirteenth year, the child was hurriedly taken
to San Lorenzo, and surreptitiously married
to Count Guido Franceschini ; she not knowing for what purpose she had accompanied her
mother to church, and after the ceremony
hurried home again with strict injunctions to
hold her peace. After a while, however, Guido
wanted his wife,—and Pietro must needs be
told ! As may be expected, the old man was
beside himself with rage—but, alas, it was then

of no avail. Some time after this, the old people were persuaded to renounce all their little property in favour of Guido ; living with him and his in the dreary old palace at Arezzo. Four months of this new life was enough for them ; they soon discovered the wickedness of the Count and his brother the Canon ; and were glad to get back to Rome, begging a living from their former neighbours and companions.

Soon after this happened, the Pope, attaining his eightieth year, proclaimed a jubilee— in which there was to be " short shrift, prompt pardon for each light offence." So Violante must needs confess *her* sin ; and, like a bolt from the blue, it startled friends and foes : the child was not hers ; she had but bought it— to please her husband, and thus save his property from strangers—of some " creature" who had found, by chance, " motherhood like a jewel in the muck."

" This fragile egg, some careless wild bird dropped
She had picked from where it waited the footfall,
And put in her own breast till broke forth finch
Able to sing God praise on mornings now."

And what excessive harm was done ? inquired Violante : and the answer is given in due course—swift and terrible ! Soon arose much hubbub among all concerned, in which the "dowry" figures as a chief factor. The matter went to the law courts, with the result that Guido can keep the dowry he had with his

wife, but must give up the other property be-
longing to Pietro.

So for the nonce the matter is apparently settled—three dreary years passing after
these events for the poor "child-wife," shut
up in the gloomy palace—years of cruelty
and terror. At the end of this period, certain complicated events happen—a brother of
the Count produced a letter, purporting to be
written by Pompilia, in which she charged her
parents with recommending her to escape with
some "gallant" from her husband. But as
the child could neither read nor write, this was
manifestly false; the charge being evidently
concocted for the purpose of enabling her husband to rid himself of his wife and yet retain the
dowry. At this time, through her husband's
brother, she meets with a young priest
Giuseppe Caponsacchi by name. At the brother's instigation, forged letters from Pompilia
pass to the Priest; her maid also brings
back letters to her mistress, explaining to
her their purport, which was that Caponsacchi "loved her." Eventually Pompilia and
the Priest meet, and she gives him to understand all that has taken place; begging him
to aid her to escape from the palace in which
she is immured. For days the priest debates
within himself as to the right or wrong of this
course; what would God have him do? But
he has seen, pitied, and loved; love comes to
his aid; and he determines to help her flee

from her husband. So, "all was determined
and performed at once," and on a certain April
evening she leaves the house, and meeting the
Priest, they journey together towards Rome.
The next morning, however, Guido awakens
somewhat later than usual, with the feeling that
he has been half poisoned ; he is soon told
what has happened ; and at once sets out in
pursuit of the fugitives, whom he overtakes
when within a stage of Rome and freedom.

For this offence the couple were tried at
Rome—the Priest sentenced to three years'
banishment at Civita ; the wife to confinement
—until she showed signs of reformation—in a
convent for Magdalens. After a while, however, Pompilia is taken ill, and consequently
placed under the care of her parents ; at whose
house, the day before Christmas, is born to
her a son, whom she names Gaetano, and who
within two days was baptized and sent away.
This event soon comes to the ears of Guido—
with the result that

> "He saw—the ins and outs to the heart of hell—
>   And took the straight line thither swift and sure."

Revenge has mastered him ; he rushes to
Vittiano, finds four " brutes of his own breed-
ing," who will follow him to the death. They
take horse, arrive in Rome on Christmas eve :

> " One,
> Struck the year's clock whereof the hours are days,
> And off was rung o' the little wheels the chime

' Good will on earth and peace to man : ' but, two
Proceeded the same bell and, evening come,
The dreadful five felt finger-wise their way
Across the town by blind cuts and black turns,
To the little lone suburban villa ; knocked—
' Who may be outside ? ' called a well-known voice,
' A friend of Caponsacchi's bringing friends
' A letter.' "

Quickly Violante opens the door—her death
was the first ; Pietro, with a sudden cry, is
next done to death ; Pompilia, though having
twenty-one wounds, being the only one not
killed. The deed of blood rouses the neigh-
bourhood ; pursuit follows ; Guido and his
accomplices are captured, and in due course
brought to trial. The usual pleadings for and
against follow ; but Guido and his accomplices are doomed.

A shot, however, was reserved. It seemed
that Guido had power to appeal to the head
of the Church, the Pope, then Innocent XII.,
which appeal is duly made : the good old Pope,
however, ultimately pronouncing the innocence
of Pompilia, and ordering the execution of
Guido and his fellows.

Such is the main drift of the story as found
in the " book " : which facts, being woven with
the " alloy " of the poet's fancy—as a " crafts-
man " in making a ring, " mingles gold with
gold's alloy," are transformed into the *Ring
and the Book.*

In the Introduction, the Poet describes the book and the manner of his finding it :

Do you see this square old yellow book, I toss
I' the air, and catch again, and twirl about
By the crumpled vellum covers—pure crude fact,
Secreted from man's life, when hearts beat hard,
And brains, high-blooded, ticked two centuries since?

And proceeds to narrate the "story." For truth's sake, he endeavoured to vouch for the facts, making inquiries at Rome for that purpose. Then we have some account of the different personages who are hereafter to speak for themselves : and herein comes the amazing fertility of the poet's genius, that the story is not once told, but is, in substance, told twelve times over—the whole forming a series of marvellous and powerful monologues, in which different phases of the same incident are repeated by different persons in drama. We have first the introduction, then the opinions of " One Half Rome," and " The Other Half Rome." " Guido " makes two long speeches, the dying Pompilia gives a record of her blameless life ; the priest, Caponsacchi, narrates his part in the terrible business ; an impartial authority, " Tertium Quid," delivers himself on the matter ; two lawyers discuss the events ; the old Pope, who had seen eighty-four summers of good and evil, gives an elaborate judgment ; and finally, the Poet, in his own person, sums up the tragic tale. It will be at once seen, what a colossal poem this

is ; but, nevertheless, the interest of the reader
is kept alive to the end. But did ever Poet
have to make such a statement as is made in
the introduction ? It is a stain which, since
the publication of this poem, has been in a
large measure wiped out, for the public have,
"after many days," had to confess that they
do like him.

"Such, British public, ye who like me not,
 (God love you !)—whom I yet have laboured for,
 Perchance more careful whoso runs may read
 Than erst when all, it seemed, could read who ran,
 Perchance more careless whoso reads may praise
 Than late when he who praised and read and wrote,—
 Was apt to find himself the selfsame me,—
 Such labour had such issue, so I wrought
 This arc, by furtherance of such alloy,
 And so, by one spirt, take away its trace
 Till, justifiably golden, rounds my ring."

The introductory portion closes with those
beautiful and pathetic lines commencing :

O lyric Love, half-angel and half-bird
And all a wonder and a wild desire,—

which read like a "dedication" to England's
great poetess, whose name, linked in that of
her husband's, will never be forgotten in the
land that gave them birth. After reading
this, let no one say that Browning is obscure,
or devoid of music. The whole passage is
charged with music, full to the brim and

overflowing—one of the most beautiful passages in English literature.

The two monologues which follow, give, in
the words of two spokesmen whom the poet is
supposed to meet, the "gossip" first of "One
Half Rome," and second of the "Other Half
Rome" on the tragedy which has been enacted.
"Half Rome" favours the husband, and lets
forth a whole torrent of evil and misery, passion
and pain. The "Other Half Rome" takes
apparently the wife's side, and reveals to us a
glimpse of the "unsoiled blue." Its opening
lines are simple in their suppressed pathos :

Another day that finds her living yet
Little Pompilia with the patient brow
And lamentable smile on those poor lips,
And, under the white hospital-array,
A flower-like body, to frighten at a bruise
You'd think, yet now, stabbed through and through
  again,
Alive i' the ruins. 'Tis a miracle !

But the monologue *Pompilia* is assuredly
the most beautiful as it is the most simple in
construction, in the book ; while the one
character in the poem, that which runs
through it like a golden thread, is the girl-
wife Pompilia. She stands on a par with
Shakespeare's women ; no poet since his time
has created such a woman as Pompilia—beautiful, sainted, true-hearted child-mother and
friend ! So real has the Poet drawn her that
we almost see her face, we recall its every tone
and touch ; and feel that we are in the

presence of as saintly a creature as ever trod earth. True nobleness is in her soul, true purity in her heart, true goodness and grace in her every action. As she lies dying in the hospital from wounds inflicted at the hands of her husband, she sobs out her last words—words of thanks to the good priest Caponsacchi who had tried to save her, and of thanks to God who had kept her pure and white. It is said, forsooth, that Browning's words are without form, rugged, devoid of music, and I know not what, by certain critics, who would educate the taste of the public down to their dead level. Listen to this; it is the patient, pure, " lily-like " child, Pompilia, who is speaking. In her last moments, with death all too visible before her, she prattles of her little baby boy, in words which show how deeply Browning can enter into the heart of a woman :

" I am just seventeen years and five months old,
And if I live one day more, three full weeks. . . .
Oh how good God is that my babe was born,—
Better than born, baptised and hid away
Before this happened, safe from being hurt !
That had been sin God could not well forgive :
He was too young to smile and save himself.

        .   .   .   .   .

            One cannot judge
Of what has been the ill or well of life,
The day that one is dying—sorrows change
Into the not altogether sorrow-like ;

I do see strangeness but scarce misery,
Now it is over, and no danger more.
My child is safe ; there seems not so much pain.
It comes, most like, that I am just absolved,
Purged of the past, the foul in me washed fair,—
One cannot both have and not have, you know,—
Being right now, I am happy and colour things.
Yes, every body that leaves life sees all
Softened and bettered : so with other sights :
To me at least was never evening yet
But seemed far beautifuller than its day,
For past is past."

So real is all this that one can easily call to mind the sad scene. The dying girl on her couch : the pale lily-like face ; the folded hands ; the quiet voice, as from another world, repeating to the awe-struck listener her sad and pathetic story. One cannot find another such picture in the wide range of English literature. See, too, how noble her faith ; how firmly she clings to God ; and how convinced she is that it was God who had sent Caponsacchi to her aid in her terrible strait :

" I answered, ' He will come.'
And, all day, I sent prayer like incense up
To God the strong, God the beneficent,
God ever mindful in all strife and strait,
Who, for our own good, makes the need extreme,
Till at the last He puts forth might and saves."

Then notice how right human, how divine is her love for her boy. It is a genuine human creature, this child-mother, that Mr. Browning has drawn for us ; not a poetical figure, but real flesh and blood, with a human beating

K

heart—strong in life, stronger in dying, and strongest in the possibilities of the Hereafter. Hear her childlike, loveable prattle about her babe, the little Gaetano:

> " My boy was born,
> Born all in love, with naught to spoil the bliss
> A whole long fortnight : in a life like mine
> A fortnight filled with bliss is long and much.
> All women are not mothers of a boy,
> Though they live twice the length of my whole life."

As for her husband, Count Guido Franceschini, the cause of the woe and misery, she cannot say a hard word for him. Pathetic, and yet full of true womanliness are the words which Pompilia speaks of her husband. For him she has no hatred, no bitterness—only an infinite pity :

> " I—pardon him ?   So far as lies in me,
> I give him for his good the life he takes. . . .
> Let him make God amends,—none, none to me.
> We shall not meet in this world nor the next,
> But where will God be absent ? In His face
> Is light, but in His shadow healing too :
> Let Guido touch the shadow and be healed ! . . .
> I could not love him, but his mother did."

But if Pompilia is the most beautiful of these monologues, Caponsacchi is assuredly the most impassioned ; while that of the Pope is the most stately and perfect in its rhythm and structure. These three monologues make up a unity of impassioned, beautiful, and stately verse. Caponsacchi tells his story with a torrent of passion, not one word but which bears the impress of truth. Especially fine is his account of the mental conflict in his spirit as to whether he shall give Pompilia the help she needs; while his description of their flight to Rome, with the account of her mind-wanderings and song-like words, is one of the greatest bits of poetic writing in our literature.

But for ripeness of experience, force and power, the monologue of the Pope stands supreme. It must be read many times, and each successive reading will deepen the impression it leaves on the mind of the reader. It is so impartial, convincing, stately. There has been nothing like it for majesty of verse since Milton wrote the " Paradise Lost." With " winter in his soul beyond the world's," Innocent XII. goes over each " dismal document " connected with the case, pleadings and counter pleadings, until the naked truth fronts him : the guilt of Guido, the innocence of Pompilia. It matters no whit to him that the chief culprit is noble, and backed up by noble friends ; nay, *that* is an added sin. He looks him through and through, but can find no redeeming point ; he sees how, in his starting in life, he had every advantage, what the world counts " sufficient help "—body and mind well balanced ; a solid intellect : wisdom and courage; all things essential to make life a success:

" Oh, and much drawback ! what where earth with-
.   out ?

Is this our ultimate stage, or starting-place
To try man's foot, if it will creep or climb,
'Mid obstacles in seeming, points that prove   ·
Advantage for who vaults from low to high
And makes the stumbling block a stepping-stone?"

Yet with all this, Guido misses the mark ; almost a priest, he rushes into sin—"believes in just the vile of life" ; even his marriage is a lie : it is lust for money, and the low appetite of the beast. So, when in his scheming, an obstacle blocks his path, the vindictive cruelty of his nature asserts itself, and he revels in the torture of a human soul : till sin is conceived to the full, and brings forth death. So does the Pope sit in judgment on the wretched man, and finds him the "mid-most blotch of black" of the evil group.

But when he comes to Pompilia, his voice changes ; an added softness tones down the stern utterance, and a smile seems to flit over the wan features. The good old Pope is *sure* of Pompilia's innocence :

> "First of the first,
> Such I pronounce Pompilia, then as now
> Perfect in whiteness—stoop thou down, my child,
> Give one good moment to the poor old Pope
> Heart-sick at having all his world to blame.
>   . . . Everywhere
> I see in the world the intellect of man
> That sword, the energy his subtle spear,
> The knowledge which defends him like a shield—
> Everywhere ; but they make not up, I think
> The marvel of a soul like thine, earth's flower,
> She holds up to the softened gaze of God ! . . .

> . . . . My flower,
> My rose, I gather for the breast of God."

As for Caponsacchi, the Pope finds much amiss and blameworthy in " this freak " of his —the masquerading in motley garb ; yet he acknowledges the " healthy rage " which animated his spirit when came the first moan from the martyr maid,—and judges him pure in thought, word, and deed. *He* knew what the temptation must have been ; but, was the temptation sharp, the trial sore ? Then, thank God, exclaims the Pope, for :

> " Why comes temptation but for man to meet
> And master and make crouch beneath his foot
> And so be pedestalled in triumph? Pray
> " Lead us into no such temptations, Lord ! "
> Yea, but, O Thou whose servants are the bold,
> Lead such temptations by the head and hair
> Reluctant dragons, up to who dares fight
> That so he may do battle and have praise !"

So he judges the matter : nowise blindly ; knowing the fallibility of human judgment, and the infirmity of the human will. He looks beyond his fallible judgment to the unerring judgment of God. Of *that* he is assured— God is, and God is true :

> " I must outlive a thing ere know it dead :
> When I outlive the faith there is a sun,
> When I lie, ashes to the very soul—
> Someone, not I, must wail above the heap,
> " He died in dark whence never morn arose.' . . .
> No,—I have light, nor fear the dark at all."

The closing lines of this monologue are intense in their realistic picturesqueness, and reveal all the massive strength of Browning's genius.

The two monologues of Guido are psychological studies in Browning's most characteristic manner. In the second speech of the Count, the man's true nature is more fully revealed. Indeed, in reading the last terrible words of Guido's, wherein he lays bare his soul to the confessors who have been sent him, one is struck with the masterful manner in which the poet-seer analyses the worldly soul of this man. He reads him through and through, and reveals to us the superstition, the undisciplined intellect, the clinging to life, the bravado of the wretched fellow. It is a wonderful portrait. Hear him, as the confessors pause, listening to his torrent of words:

" Come, I am tired of silence !   Pause enough !
You have prayed : I have gone inside my soul
And shut its door behind me ; 'tis your torch
Makes the place dark,—the darkness let alone
Grows tolerable twilight. .   .   .   .
You never know what life means till you die :
Even throughout life, 'tis death that makes life live,
Gives it whatever the significance."

But at the last he breaks down. Life is sweet after all ; his bravado is gone ; the whole contemptible cowardice of his nature bursts forth—and in his last words he proves

the innocence of his wife by invoking her aid
to save him :

"Who are these you have let descend my stair ?
Ha, their accursed psalm !   Lights at the sill !
Is it " Open" they dare bid. you ?   Treachery !
Sirs, have I spoken one word all this while
Out of the world of words I had to say ?
Not one word !   All was folly—I laughed and mocked !
Sirs, my first true word, all truth and no lie,
Is—save me notwithstanding ! Life is all !
I was just stark mad—let the madman live
Pressed by as many chains as you please pile !
Do n't open ! Hold me from them !   I am yours,
I am the Grand-duke's—no, I am the Pope's !
Abate—Cardinal—Christ—Maria—God, . . .
Pompilia, will you let them murder me ? "

In the concluding section, the Poet gives a
final summing up of the matter.   First we have
a letter from a stranger, a Venetian visitor at
Rome, who writes on the evening of the exe-
tution of Guido and his accomplices, and who
gives a description of that event.   Guido's
friend, Don Giacinto Arcangeli, also writes on
the same evening ; followed by an epistle from
the " tall blue-eyed Fisc whose head is capped
with cloud," Doctor Bottini.   The Doctor en-
closes in his letter the report of a sermon by
the Augustinian monk, from the text, " Let
God be true and every man a liar,"—and here
the reader will find one of Browning's most
eloquent passages.   The Poet then sums up
the whole :

"So did this old woe fade from memory,
  Till after, in the fulness of the days,
  I needs must find an ember yet unquenched
  And, breathing, blow the spark to flame. It lives,
  If precious be the soul of man to man.
  So, British Public, who may like me yet,
  (Marry and amen !) learn one lesson hence
  Of many which whatever lives should teach :
  This lesson, that our human speech is nought,
  Our human testimony false, our frame
  And human estimation words and wind."

Such are the main features of the *Ring and the Book*, and I hope enough has been said to prove to the student the wealth, wonder, and intense human interest of this poem. It must be read and re-read, pondered and thought over ; for it is a decided addition to our human experience. Certainly, it is a formidable task to put before a "beginner" in the study of Browning,—a poem, consisting of upwards of 21,000 lines. But the reader will be amply repaid for his assiduity ; he will have seen a woeful tragedy put before him in an altogether new form ; he will have felt the beat and sway of passion and pain, hate and fear, hope and joy ; and he will have seen human hearts laid bare before the analytical power of this most incisive and masterful of modern poets.

VIII.

AND now, in bringing this little work to a
close I trust I may have made, to the student
at any rate, somewhat clearer the depth of
thought and power of inspiration to be found
in the works of him whom I take to be the
Chief Poet of our Age ; chief, because *he*, more
than any other, perceived the needs and
yearnings of this restless period, and set himself to supply them. He never aimed at
popularity; success was in nowise his ambi-
tion : he was content with the judgment of
his peers, and could afford to wait the verdict
of the populace. "Were you never discouraged," I asked him once, "at the indifference of the public and the hostility of the
critics to your writings ?" "*Never*," was his
emphatic reply. "Why, I had the approba-
tion of Fox, of Mill, of Forster, and I was
content with *their* verdict." It has been well
for us that he was so content, and went on his
high career regardless of the public indifference
or the critics' hostility. Had he so chosen
he might, early in his career, have obtained a
popularity as large and widespread as that of
his great contemporary : for he had a unique
lyric power, and in ballad writing was easily

L

great. On these lines, he might have speedily·
achieved popularity; but this was not his
work—and this would not have won him the
title of Chief Poet of the Age.

I hold him to be "chief" also because he, of
all modern writers, so largely combined the
prophetic, or the *seeing* power, and this it is
that places him far above more melodious-
voiced singers. This poet deals with the philo-
sophical and intellectual problems of his day;
he is a great religious teacher; he influenced
men's actions and lives—in a word, he was a
seer. To him the world was alive and radiant
with hope; he never lost his hold on God,
never faltered in his high ideals of life, never
failed in his belief in humanity. God's father-
hood was to him an assured fact—and equally
assured was his certainty of Immortality. His
death was as noble as his life—it was the
triumph hour of his career: surrounded by
those to whom he was bound by the tenderest
of all ties, he heard across the waters that
beat against the walls of the Palazzo
Rezzonico, the "well done" of his compatriots
in the land of his birth; and his hands had
held for a moment the volume containing the
last fruits of his brain and heart. Full of
trust in the Future, he passed the veil into the
Unseen—his latest utterance testifying to the
greatness of his hope:

At the midnight in the silence of the sleep-time,
  When you set your fancies free,

Will they pass to where—by death, fools think, im-
prisoned—
Low he lies who once so loved you, whom you loved so,
—Pity me?

. . . .

No, at noonday in the bustle of man's work-time
Greet the unseen with a cheer!
Bid him forward, breast and back, as either should be,
"Strive and thrive!" cry "Speed—fight on, fare ever
There as here!"

And herein lies his power to influence yet
further the England he loved so well—for
Robert Browning is emphatically the poet of
the future. Dreadful things are prophesied of
the coming age—and the pessimists are hold-
ing high carnival over the downfall of the old
creeds: but the foundations are firm still, it
is only the building that is changing, not the
superstructure. Faith is still alive, and uplift-
ing the hearts of men; religion is still doing
her beneficent work, as it has never done it
before, but bigotry and intolerance are passing away; superstition is dead, but Christ is
alive, and the new age is pregnant with a
tolerant, large-hearted, all-embracing Christianity, broad as the wide waters of the
moon-swayed Atlantic. Of this new age
Robert Browning will be the great high-priest
and poet, the inspired leader and teacher.
Carlyle tells us that some familiar verses of
Göethe's sound to him like the marching song
of humanity, but Browning has written for us
our marching song, and, in his poem of the
Grammarian's Funeral, he leads us on, step

by step, till we gain the mountain heights. It
is an account of the burial of a learned man,
who loved learning for learning's sake, seeking
payment, not from man, but God. As his
friends carry his body, for burial, up to the top
of the mountain crest, they chant their uplift-
ing song,—in words that haunt the memory,
lifting the spirit above the world's turmoils,
into that serener atmosphere where human
hearts beat in unison with the heart of the
Father:

Oh, if we draw a circle premature
    Heedless of far gain,
Greedy for quick returns of profit, sure
    Bad is our bargain!
Was it not great? did not he throw on God
    (He loves the burthen)—
God's task to make the heavenly period
    Perfect the earthen? . . . .

That low man seeks a little thing to do,
    Sees it and does it:
This high man, with a great thing to pursue,
    Dies ere he knows it.
That low man goes on adding one to one,
    His hundred's soon hit:
This high man, aiming at a million,
    Misses an unit.
That, has the world here—should he need the next,
    Let the world mind him!
This, throws himself on God, and unperplext
    Seeking shall find Him!

S. & J. Brawn, Printers, 13, Gate Street, High Holborn, London.